ENGAGED TO MR. RIGHT

A FAKE MARRIAGE ROMANCE

LILIAN MONROE

1

MAX

I TAKE a deep breath before I squat down. I brace myself for the inevitable burning daggers of pain that will go through my knee when it bends. I know they're coming. A bead of sweat dribbles between my shoulder blades, and I try not to let my apprehension show on my face.

My pretty, sympathetic physical therapist is watching me. Naomi's big green eyes are glued on my knees, and her eyebrows are pulled ever so slightly together. The alabaster skin on her forehead, usually so smooth, is ever so slightly creased as she watches me.

A second ticks by and her sharp, green eyes flick up to mine. I can see the patient encouragement in her face.

Whenever you're ready, she's saying. I don't feel ready. I blink, blowing the air out of my nostrils.

I guess I'd better go for it.

Ready for the pain, I bend at the knees and start squatting. My joints bend, my ankles flex, and the bead of sweat makes its way down my spine towards the waistband of my athletic shorts.

Down I go, deeper and deeper into my squat. I'm holding

my breath, ready for the moment when the knee flexion will reach the point of agony.

Before I know it, I'm in a full squat. Naomi's face breaks into a huge smile and my heart flips. My eyes widen and she starts laughing.

"Good work, Max!" She says, reaching her arms out towards me. I grab her hands, using her support to come back up.

"What...?" I can't even finish my sentence. I bend down again, holding onto her hands and squatting almost down to the floor. I spring back up, my jaw hanging open. "There's no pain!"

Naomi pulls her hands from mine and claps excitedly. I smile despite myself. There's a slight tingling in my fingers where they were touching hers, but I try to ignore it. She looks like she's almost happy enough to jump up and down.

The sun is shining through the window, making her red hair look like it's made of pure fire. It's pulled back from her face in a high pony tail, setting off the soft angles of her face. For a moment, I wonder what it would look like if her hair tumbled down around her face.

"You've made such great progress," she exclaims. "You've been doing your exercises, haven't you?"

"I have, actually," I say, surprised.

"I can tell. I'm like a dentist who always knows whether or not you've been flossing," she laughs.

I grin, bending my knee with wonder. When I started seeing Naomi three months ago, I thought it would be just another waste of time and money. Unexpectedly, she's guided me through a new, comprehensive physical therapy plan and now my knee is finally starting to feel normal again.

It hasn't felt this good since before the injury happened. That was almost four years ago, but it feels like it happened yesterday. The pain in my knee is a constant reminder of what I lost.

One bad tackle during my college football championship and I lost everything. I lost my football career, I lost my girlfriend, I lost my identity. I went from star quarterback, drafted to the NFL, to a washed-up nobody with a sore knee.

Every ligament in my knee was torn when I was tackled that day, but it was more than a knee joint that was ruined. It was my life.

And now, as pathetic as it feels to be proud of squatting down without pain, it actually feels *good*. Naomi is beaming, and I feel proud. I feel like myself again.

"Good," she says. "Hop up here." She pats the massage table beside us, kicking the step-stool towards it. I use the stool to sit on the table, swinging my legs up to lie down.

My eyes follow her, and I notice the way her blue, shapeless polo shirt clings to her curves. It has the words 'Physio-FIT' across the back. She bends down to pick up a long rubber loop, stringing it over a hook on the wall. Her yoga pants make her ass look perfectly perky.

I noticed how attractive she was during our first appointment, but suddenly it feels like my body has woken up from a long slumber. Watching her move is sending blood to parts of my body that should not have blood rushing to them right now.

Maybe I was too focused on the pain in my knee, or too focused on the fact that my injury would never get better for my body to react to her attractiveness. She turns back towards me and nods to the table.

I know the drill. I lie on my back as Naomi stands beside me. I wish I was wearing something with a bit more coverage than these loose athletic shorts.

"So how's work going?" She grabs my ankle and bends my

leg as I stare at the ceiling. She's gentle but pushes me at the same time, moving my knee back towards my chest until I start to feel the first twinges of pain.

"It's fine," I respond through gritted teeth. Naomi straightens my leg again.

"Yeah?" She bends my knee again, straightening it up in the air and hooking it onto her shoulder. She places her hand on the table next to my chest and curls her other arm around my leg. She leans forward, bracing herself against me as she stretches my leg up towards the ceiling. A strand of hair falls across her forehead.

Her lips are full and pink, and they're stretched in a determined line. I groan as she stretches me, trying to ignore the heat that's spreading through my stomach.

Why am I turned on right now?

I mean, I know why. I mean why *right now*?

I stare at the ceiling again, shifting all my attention to memorize the shape of a water stain on one of the ceiling tiles.

"Yeah, work's good," I finally respond. "We just landed a big contract with the government."

"The one you told me about a couple weeks ago?" She asks, her hand drifting down to the crook of my hip as she stretches my leg up further. I try to ignore the thought of her slender, soft fingers so close to my crotch.

I clear my throat. "Yeah, that one. It took a long time to get past all the approvals and red tape, but they've agreed to let us supply the materials for one of their big construction projects down the coast."

"That's great!" Naomi answers, dropping my leg down. "On your stomach."

I turn on my stomach and my heart starts thumping because I know what's coming. I hear her squirt some oil onto her hands and I'm grateful that I've turned around. At least if my body decides to...*misbehave...* it'll be hidden against the massage table.

When her oiled hands touch my leg, I forget what I was saying. It's simultaneously painful and exciting as she kneads my hamstring and around my knee. How have I never felt like this before? I've never even *thought* of Naomi this way. She was just one of the many members of the team that are supposed to get my knee back to normal.

But right now, as her hands move further up my leg, this feels *very* different from the other times.

Maybe it's because the shooting pain that's usually associated with these physical therapy massages isn't there today.

"How does that feel?" Naomi asks as if she can read my mind. "You're not complaining as much as usual."

I can hear the grin in her voice. "Complaining!" I say, turning my head to catch her eye.

She's laughing to herself, kneading my hamstring a little bit harder as I yelp.

"You did that on purpose." There's a gleam in her eye when she glances at me, and a shiver passes through me.

"I'm just trying to get you better, Mr. Westbrook," she retorts. "I'm glad to see you're improving."

"You're going to injure me again with those hands of yours," I grumble. But she won't. I love what her hands are doing to me.

I love it a lot... maybe too much. My heart thumps.

What is going on?

Her hands move over my shorts and she starts digging her elbow into my ass. I groan.

"Your glutes are still tight," she remarks. "Have you been using the ball I gave you?"

"It's too painful," I whine. I know I sound like a child, but I can't help it.

"You need to loosen your glutes up, Max," she reproaches. "Right here," she notes, poking the side of my ass. "This muscle is pulling along here," her hand drifts along the side of my leg towards my knee.

My cock pulses, and my heart races.

Thank *fuck* I'm laying on my stomach.

Naomi doesn't seem to notice. "If you don't loosen that up, it'll keep pulling sideways at your knee and it'll be difficult to get the right alignment in your knee joint. It's important."

"Right," I groan as she digs her elbow back in my ass.

"It's very common when people have had a total ACL and MCL reconstruction. We need to make sure everything aligns properly for you to heal."

"I thought I was making good progress," I grumble, turning my head again to look at her. "Aren't you supposed to be telling me how great I'm doing?"

She stops massaging me, putting her hands on her hips and raising an eyebrow.

"I'm *supposed* to be getting you better, Max. I'm not going to tell you what you want to hear just to make you happy. Five minutes with the ball. Loosen your glutes up every morning like I showed you."

There's a gleam in her eye, and her lip quirks up a tiny bit.

"If you don't like it, find another physio. It won't hurt my feelings."

"No," I respond. "I think I'll stick with you. You've got those great sharp elbows," I groan as she goes back to work on my glutes.

Naomi laughs. She works on the other side of my body, and after a few minutes she finally pats my leg.

"Your torture is over, Max. Good work today."

I sit up and swing my legs over the side of the massage table. I try not to stare at the curve of her hip, or the way her yoga pants are stretched across her ass.

She turns back to me and tucks a strand of hair behind her ear, smiling.

"See you next week! You need any help getting out?"

I shake my head, grunting. "I'm good. See you next week."

I watch her walk towards her office, hypnotized by the movement of her ass from side to side with every step. When she finally moves out of view, I shake my head and grab my stuff, heading towards the locker rooms.

Once I'm dressed for work, I put my tie on in the mirror, staring at myself for a few seconds. I shake my head. I need to get it together. Naomi is the best physical therapist I've had. I had the second operation on my knee two years ago, and this is the best I've felt since I was in college.

I can't—no, I *won't*—mess it up by hitting on her. There are plenty of other women to chase.

I bend my knee, waiting for the familiar crackles and pops that usually accompany any movement. There aren't any, and I take a deep breath.

I definitely can't mess this up. As attractive as she is, I need to think about my knee.

For the first time since the injury happened and my football career ended, I actually feel like myself again.

2

NAOMI

"You're blushing."

"I am *not!*" I turn away from Meghan as my cheeks start to burn. I know I'm red—I can feel the blush creeping up my neck and covering my cheeks. Even my ears feel hot. I probably look like a Christmas bulb right now.

"You are *so* blushing right now."

Her dark eyebrow arches gracefully as she watches me. I roll my eyes.

"What if I am?"

"He's a player," she says, glancing towards the front door. "Max Westbrook is in the tabloids every second day. Do you know he left his fiancée at the altar? Literally *at the altar*. He just didn't show up."

"Poor woman," I reply, shaking my head. "That must have been mortifying."

"You can say that again," Meghan grumbles, turning to face me. She leans her tall, slender body against her desk as I start wrapping up some resistance bands to put them away.

"So what's going on between you two, anyway? There was lots of laughing going on for a simple physio session."

"What, I'm not allowed to enjoy my job?"

"Not that much," she retorts, grinning.

I try to swallow back the blush that threatens to light up my face again. I shake my head. "He's making good progress, and I'm happy about it. When he first came in here he could hardly bend his knee. Now he's squatting with no pain!"

"Must be all that dedicated, one-on-one work you're doing."

"Shut up, Meg," I laugh. "*Nothing* is going on. He's my client, and I would never do anything with a client. Plus, he's not my type."

Meg snorts, pushing herself off the desk and grabbing a protein bar from the shelf. She walks a couple steps and turns back towards me, unwrapping the bar and taking a bite. She points the protein bar at me and shakes her head.

"Max Westbrook is *everyone's* type. Be careful."

"Don't worry."

She stares at me for a few seconds, and I force myself to hold her gaze. Finally, she shrugs. "You decide what you're wearing on Saturday?"

I sigh, leaning my head back and closing my eyes.

Shit. Saturday.

Meghan makes a noise, and I can almost *hear* the smirk on her face. "You forgot, didn't you?"

"Maybe," I reply, turning towards her. Yep—she's smirking.

"It's our boss's *bachelorette party*, Naomi!"

"Yeah, well, I'm not really a 'wedding' person. Why are we invited, anyway? It's not like we're friends with her."

Meg grins. "Maybe we are her friends, and we just don't know it."

"At least she said it would be on the company credit card."

"So I take it that's a 'no' to the question about what you're going to wear?"

"I don't know, I'll wear jeans and a nice top, or something."

"Wow, way to narrow it down." She takes another bite of her protein bar. "Come over in the afternoon on Saturday. Ariana's coming too."

"Does Julia even know her?"

"Company credit card," Meg laughs. "She's crashing the bachelorette party."

"Typical Ari," I laugh.

"Come on, come over. We can get nice and buzzed beforehand and I'll help you get ready. I have a couple dresses that you could try on."

"I don't think your clothes will fit me," I say, glancing at her tall, willowy frame. My hands drift to my wide hips and I shake my head. "I'm about four inches shorter than you and a couple sizes bigger."

"You are not," she says, rolling her eyes. "You just always wear clothes that are a couple sizes too big for you. Show off those curves, Naomi! You're a knockout. Plus, you need to get laid, if only to stop going gaga over your freaking clients."

"Mm," I reply, turning to my desk and finding Max's file. I can sense Meg's eyes on my back so I turn to look over my shoulder. "*Fine.*"

A grin spreads over her face. "Good. I'm going for lunch. You coming?"

"Gotta finish this paperwork. See you when you get back."

Meg makes a noise and glides through the door. I watch her leave before sinking down into a chair. Closing my eyes for a moment, I drop my head into my hand.

I open my eyes and stare at the stack of papers in front of me. Before I know what I'm doing, I trace his name with my fingers: Max Westbrook.

Meg is way too perceptive. I *was* laughing more than usual, and it wasn't because Max was making progress. It was the way he was looking at me. More than once, I got lost in those deep, blue eyes of his. I had my hands all over him—I mean, I had to. It's my job! But this time, it wasn't like his other appointments. When I was massaging his leg, it was sending thrills through my body that are still echoing through me now.

My hands drift down to my thighs and I remember the way his hard, muscled body looked and felt as he laid on my massage table.

I take a deep breath and put the stack of papers down. I jot down a few notes and file them away, shaking my head.

Meg is right. Max Westbrook is my client. Not only that, he's a super rich, super out-of-my-league playboy. No matter how electrifying his touch is, or how deep and blue his eyes are, I can't get involved.

I snort at the thought, shaking my head. Get involved? It's not like I have the choice. He wasn't exactly coming on to me or anything. He just *looked* at me, for crying out loud. And here I am, losing my mind over it.

I stare through the door and take a deep breath. Meg is right. I *do* need to get laid, if only to stop myself from going wobbly-kneed every time an attractive man walks through the door.

The last thing I need is to get distracted. There are dozens of attractive, athletic men who walk through these doors. Professional athletes come here with injuries all the time. Working here is a privilege, and I can't forget that. Not even if Max sends a thrill through my body every time he's near.

That's just part of the job.

... Right?

3

MAX

A CAN of beer hits me in the chest before I even know it's coming. I catch it as it tumbles down my stomach, looking up to see who threw it.

"What's up with you, Max?" Joel cocks his head to the side. "Bad day at work?"

Monday Night Football is blaring on Joel's TV, and he sits down in his plushy recliner as he waits for me to answer. I shift on the couch, the leather creaking underneath me. I shrug as I stare at the can of beer in my hands.

"Gonna be a long week, I guess."

Joel grunts in acknowledgement. He brushes a strand of sandy blonde hair off his forehead and tips his beer back. When he wipes his mouth on his sleeve, he stares at me with those sharp, pale brown eyes of his and I try not to shift in my seat.

I haven't been thinking about work at all—I've been thinking about *her*. About Naomi. About the way her hands had been all over my legs, and the way her skin had glowed, even under the stark fluorescent lights of her office. I'd been thinking about the tremor that had passed through my chest when she smiled at me. It was right when I squatted down without pain for the first time in years.

I jump when Joel speaks again, and I know the reaction hasn't gone unnoticed. As boisterous as Joel can be, he can read me like a book.

"How was your physio appointment? You look like you're doing really well since you changed physical therapists. You're not complaining about your fucking knee every five minutes anymore."

I'm going to choose to ignore that.

"It was good," I answer, keeping my eyes glued on the TV. I can feel Joel's stare, and I know my best friend can tell there was more to the appointment than it just being 'good'.

But right now, as I sit down for our regular Monday hang-out, I don't want to talk about it. I don't want to explain that I had the hots for my physical therapist. I don't want to laugh along to his jokes and brush off my attraction to her.

I make the mistake of glancing at my best friend. I see the gleam in his eyes as he arches his eyebrow. He cracks open a new beer and takes a sip, never taking his eyes off me. I chuckle, shaking my head.

I know an inquisition is coming.

I'll have to field his questions and pretend like I didn't get turned on today. I'll have to pretend like Naomi is no one, like I haven't been thinking about her all day.

Joel opens his mouth, and I know the barrage of questions is coming.

I'm saved by a knock on the door. Our friends, Graham and Connor, come tumbling through the door.

"Yo!" Graham calls out, marching towards us.

"What's up?" Joel responds.

I grunt, cracking open the beer that Joel threw at me. It

sprays out, fizzing and bubbling all over me as soon as I crack it open. I'm greeted by a chorus of laughs. I glance at Joel.

"You dickhead," I grin.

He throws his hands up. "What! I didn't do anything."

Connor chortles and slaps me on the shoulder, dropping down to sit next to me on the couch. "Never trust a beer that Joel gets for you. Didn't you learn anything in college?"

"Apparently not," I laugh.

Graham drops a bag of chips on the coffee table, and my shoulders relax. Amid the comfortable conversation, the ribbing and joking, the easy friendship between the four of us, I forget about my day. I forget about how completely off-balance I felt earlier, and how my mind keeps circling back to my appointment.

The conversation turns to football.

"I keep telling myself that the Giants should lose to get a high draft pick, but then they go and play like this today and I can't help but feel great," Joel says, shaking his head.

"Losing never feels good," I respond, sipping my beer. My shirt is still soaked with the spray, but I don't really care. "I remember the day we lost the championship in college. Losing was almost worse than busting up my knee."

Silence hangs between us as we all take a sip.

Finally, Graham grunts. "That was fucking tough, man." He runs a hand through his black hair and purses his lips as he stares at me.

"Yeah."

Joel glances over at me. He lifts a finger to point at me. "You know, that's the first time in four years I've heard you talk about your injury without being asked."

I straighten my leg out in front of me, massaging my quad muscle and staring at my knee. I shrug.

"Yeah?"

"Yeah," Connor says. "Usually whenever anyone mentions it you go all quiet."

"Huh," I respond, not knowing what else to say. They're right, obviously. I never talk about my knee, and I never talk about that day on the football field when my life changed forever.

"It's gotta be a girl," Graham says, grinning. "Who is she?"

"What?" I say, frowning. "No!"

Joel laughs, grabbing a chip from the bag on the table. "I fucking knew it!" He crunches down on the chip and then brushes his fingers across his shirt to wipe the orange dust from them. He shakes his head, laughing. "Fucking finally."

"What do you mean, finally?!" I protest.

"You haven't really liked any women since... you know," Connor answers, wiggling his eyebrows. His brown eyes are shining as he opens them wide. "Since *she who shall not be named* was around."

"Who, Farrah? I've been with girls since her!" I avoid their stares, choosing instead to sip my beer. It's true! I've been with lots of women since my ex left me after I got injured. "I was fucking engaged!"

"Yeah, but you haven't actually *liked* any of them. Even Heather," Graham laughs. "Best decision you ever made, not to marry her. I'm not even sure you really liked her."

I grunt, remembering the torturous months leading up to my failed engagement.

Connor nudges me. "Come on, who is she?"

I glance at the three of them, trying to keep my face steady.

"I don't know what any of you are talking about. There's no one."

A grin spreads over Joel's face. He leans forward, a strand

of blonde hair falling across his forehead. He shakes his head slowly from side to side.

"It's your physio, isn't it."

"I don't know what you're talking about."

"I knew it!" He laughs triumphantly, turning to Connor and Graham. "He was acting all weird earlier, but it wasn't until you said it was a girl that it all made sense. Is that why you've been making such good progress with your knee lately?"

"Shut up, Joel," I grumble as I feel three sets of eyes boring into me.

"She hot?" Connor asks.

"She's gotta be, you know how Max is," Graham responds with a laugh. "He only goes for perfect tens. You got a picture of her?"

"My ankle is kind of sore, maybe I should make an appointment," Joel laughs.

"God, shut the fuck up you guys. I'm not seeing her! I don't even know her!"

"So you've just got a little crush on your physio but you're too shy to ask her out? That's cute," Graham grins.

"Game's back on," I grunt in relief, and the four of us turn back to the TV.

I drain the rest of my beer and crush the can in my hand. My mind reels. I feel like I've just run a marathon. My heart is racing and I'm vaguely mad at my friends, but I also know they're right. I do have a crush on her. I mean, she's an attractive woman—how could I *not* notice that?

Maybe it's the fact that she's making my knee feel better that draws me to her. She's making me feel like the old 'me'. She's giving me my life back. A life without pain and creaky knees. A life where maybe, I'll be able to play football again.

4

NAOMI

By the time Saturday comes around, our boss, Julia, has talked the whole office's ear off about her bachelorette party. At least Meg has stopped teasing me about Max Westbrook.

Mostly.

"Imagine if Max saw you like *this*," Meg whistles when I walk out of the bathroom. She wiggles her eyebrows. I laugh, rolling my eyes. My hands fly to my hair to smooth it down, and I glance at myself in the hallway mirror. I shake my head.

"Stop it."

"He'd be *begging* you to give him all *kinds* of physio."

"Oh my God, Meg, shut up!" I laugh as a blush stains my cheeks. "You're the worst."

"And by the worst, you mean the best, right?"

"I'm just glad Meg's attention is off me," our friend, Ariana, calls out from the kitchen. "I couldn't take all the teasing about Mason."

She appears with two glasses of white wine, handing one to me and the other to Meg.

"I'm not done with you and Mason," Meg laughs. "Just momentarily occupied."

"Well 'momentarily occupy' yourself with something else," I retort. The two of them laugh. Ariana ducks back into the kitchen and grabs herself a glass, and then we clink them all together.

"In all honesty, Naomi," Meg says, "you look like a knock-out. You should wear green more often, it makes your eyes and your hair look *insane*."

"Thanks for lending me this." I run my fingers down the silky fabric covering my hips. "It's gorgeous."

"Keep it," Meg says with a wave of her hand. "It doesn't fit me properly anyways. I've never even worn it. I don't have your body."

"Meg," I start, shaking my head. "You're like, the definition of a perfect ten. You look like a supermodel."

"If we're just standing around handing out compliments, when do I get a turn?" Ariana laughs. She drops onto the couch and drains half her glass of wine in one sip.

"You have enough men following you around like lost puppies showering you with compliments," Meg shoots back, cocking her hip to the side and arching her eyebrow. "How many boyfriends do you have right now? I lost track."

Ariana grins. "*None*, thank you very much. I've taken a vow of celibacy."

A short moment of silence precedes riotous laughter exploding out of all three of us. Meg goes to the speaker and plugs in her phone, putting on some music. I sit down next to Ariana, letting her top off my glass while Meg starts dancing on the coffee table.

We polish off two bottles of wine before heading out the door to meet Julia.

By the time we make it to the bar, Julia and the rest of her friends are there. By the look of it, they're on their second or third round already. We show up just in time to be handed a shot of something blue, and get a stumbling hug from our boss. She's wearing a thrift-store veil and a sash that says 'Bride-to-Be.'

I exchange a glance with Ariana, who just shrugs and takes the shot. She leans over towards me as I stare suspiciously at the blue liquid.

"Come on, Naomi," she half-shouts into my ear over the music. "You need to loosen up a little. When was the last time you got laid?"

I hate how easily I blush, especially in moments like these. Ariana laughs.

"I rest my case."

I roll my eyes and knock the shot back. Ariana cheers, and Julia reappears with an armful of sashes.

"Put these on," she shouts as the music thumps. I take one, glancing at Meg and Ariana.

"'Bride Tribe'," Meg reads. She grins at me and then shrugs. "I guess that's us."

We shrug into the silly sashes and Julia hugs us again. As much as I resisted coming, I can't deny how happy she looks. She waves her head back and forth and plays with her veil as she takes another shot. Her other friends lean in for a picture and everyone laughs and hugs.

I look down at my 'Bride Tribe' sash and feel a pang in my chest.

I never really believed in weddings. My mother never married, and I don't even know who my father is. She raised me to be independent, and I always thought that marriage was an institution designed to keep women in their place.

But now, I watch Julia, and I wonder if that's true. She runs a successful physical therapy practice, and she's a great boss. And yet, here she is, getting drunk and celebrating how happy she is to be getting married. Is it possible to have it both ways?

Meg hands me a drink as we watch them screaming and dancing.

"Sickening, isn't it," she says to me.

I grin, shrugging. "I don't know, it's kind of nice. She looks really happy."

"She looks really *drunk*," Meg corrects. "And just because you have a crush on some rich ex-football star, don't go all gooey on me."

I dig my elbow into her ribs as she laughs, throwing her arm around me. "Come on, let's dance," she says. "It would be rude not to."

We elbow our way onto the dance floor, forming a circle around Julia. We sway and laugh and dance as the joy becomes contagious. I can't help but be happy for Julia.

Meg turns towards me and dances with me, clinking her glass against mine. I grin and take a sip, when she looks over her shoulder. Her jaw drops and my heart starts beating. Meg glances back at me, nodding her chin behind me as she arches her eyebrow.

She doesn't need to say anything, because I already know who it is. Whether it was the expression on her face, or if I could just *sense* him behind me, I know it's him.

Max Westbrook.

The music gets quieter as I turn around, and people seem to be moving in slow motion as our eyes lock. His eyes are bluer than I remembered. He takes a step towards me, gliding through the crowd of dancers like a shark through a school of fish.

His eyes roam over my body, sending delicious tingles coursing through my veins. His dark hair is pushed back from his broad forehead, and his black t-shirt is pulled tight across his muscular chest. I ball my hands into fists to stop myself from reaching out and touching him.

He looks a lot better in those jeans than he does in athletic shorts.

A *lot* better.

When he's in front of me, I inhale his scent and another thrill passes through me. He leans forward and his cheek brushes against mine as his hand drifts to my hip. He lays a soft kiss on my cheek and says hello.

I melt.

I close my eyes as the smell of man fills my nostrils.

"Bride Tribe?" He asks, pulling away and arching his eyebrow as a grin stretches his lips.

I laugh, shrugging and pointing my thumb over my shoulder towards Julia. She's found a condom somewhere, and is slingshotting it across the dance floor to a chorus of shrieks and laughs. Max nods, grinning.

"Ah."

"Yeah," I reply.

"You want to get some air?" He nods to the front door of the bar.

"Yeah," I say. I can't seem to manage any actual words. I glance back at Meg, who is staring at me with a big grin on her face. Ariana is right beside her, giving me a not-so-subtle thumbs-up. I shake my head, turning back towards Max. He slips his hand into mine as if it were the most natural thing in the world and guides me towards the exit.

5

MAX

OF ALL THE BARS, in all of New York City, she walks into mine. Or I walk into hers. Or we both walk into the same one. Whatever.

This isn't Casablanca, it's real life. And right now, Naomi Rose's hand is clasped in mine as we walk out of the crowded space. The fresh air hits us as soon as the door opens. It's the end of September, and the chill has well and truly set into the air in New York City. Naomi takes a deep breath, slipping her hand out of mine and running her fingers through her fiery red hair.

"It's hot in there." I watch her chest rise and fall as she fans her face, flicking her eyes back towards me. Her look almost knocks me back. I don't know if it's her makeup, or hair, or that emerald green, skin-tight dress she has on, but looking at her is doing all kinds of things to my body.

"It is," I reply, trying not to stare at her. I nod to her sash. "Whose idea were those?"

Naomi runs her finger along the sash, looking down at the gold writing. She chuckles, shrugging. "Not mine."

"Not into weddings?"

"Not into marriage, really," she replies with an arch of her eyebrow.

"No? I thought girls loved weddings."

Naomi rolls her eyes, planting a hand on her hip. "Right, because all women are just one monolith who share all thoughts and opinions."

"That's not what I meant," I grin.

"That's a stupid stereotype anyways."

"What's that?"

"The one where women are all these wedding-crazy bridezillas who plan their wedding from the day they're born."

"I've met lots of women who love weddings."

Naomi huffs, shaking her head. It feels like the wedding talk has struck a nerve, but I don't know how to steer the conversation away from it.

"I've met lots of *men* who want to get married," she says. "It takes two to tango, you know. I refuse to believe that all these men are just being dragged to the altar against their will."

"True."

"I hate that 'ball and chain' saying. If you don't want to get married, then don't get married! It shouldn't be joked about like it's a life sentence. Why is there so much pressure on us to tie the knot?"

"You should talk to my parents," I laugh. "Maybe you could convince them to come around."

She glances at me, cocking that pretty head to the side. Her eyes soften.

"Do they pressure you to get married?"

I snort, glancing down the street as a car zooms past. I rub my hands together to warm them up as I shake my head.

"They're brutal. They've been asking me when I'm going to get married since I left for college."

"That makes me glad my mom is the way she is," Naomi replies, following my gaze to the street. I steal a glance at her and my chest squeezes. Her body looks unbelievable in that dress. It makes her skin look milky white and her hair look like it's made of pure fire.

I clear my throat as the heat flows between my legs. "Your mom's not into marriage?"

Naomi snorts, looking at me. Her eyes are gleaming under the streetlights. She tucks a strand of hair behind her ear, shaking her head.

"My mom is pressuring me *not* to get married."

"Must be nice."

"I guess," Naomi laughs. "She never got married, and I think she instilled this idea in me that marriage was a way to keep women under control."

"Do you believe that?"

Naomi is quiet for a while, and I take a step closer to her. She shivers, and I run my hands over her arms. She must be freezing in that dress.

She closes her eyes and lets out a soft sigh that makes my body thrum with desire. When she opens her eyes again, she tilts her chin up to look at me. Her lips look soft and kissable and her tongue darts out to lick them. I resist the urge to groan.

"No," she finally responds. "I don't believe that marriage is evil. I think it's not for everyone, but I do think that people can get married for love and that it can work. But I think that people rush into it."

"You can say that again."

My hands are still on her arms, and the touch is making my heart beat faster. I desperately want to kiss her. I want her to flick those pretty, green eyes up at me, and I want to crush my lips against hers.

"Why did you leave your fiancée at the altar?" She asks, looking up at me as her eyebrows draw together. I drop my hands and take a deep breath.

My failed engagement is like a constant reminder of how things just never seem to work out for me. It didn't work out in college, when I thought I would marry Farrah. And then it didn't work out again two years later, when I realized I couldn't spend my life with Heather.

Maybe the problem is with me, not them.

Naomi is still waiting for an answer, so I shrug.

"I guess it's just what you were saying. We rushed into it. I gave in to the pressure from my parents. I thought it was the right thing, and then I realized it wasn't. Or maybe she wasn't the right woman."

"And it didn't occur to you before the day of your wedding? I mean that poor woman..."

"I know, I'm an asshole."

Naomi grins. "I never said that." She shivers again, and I wish I had a jacket to lend her. Instead, I just wrap my arms around her and pull her close. She sighs into me, leaning her head against my chest. My heart is thumping, and I hope she can't hear it.

"You want to go back inside?"

"Not really," she mumbles into my chest. "But I guess we should."

"I thought you weren't the kind of woman who does things just because you think you should. Isn't that what all the hatred of weddings is about?"

Something flashes in her eyes as a grin spreads across her face. She pushes away from me, keeping her hands on my chest. "Mr. Westbrook, if I didn't know any better, I'd think you were mocking me."

"Me? Never."

She takes a step back, searching my face. Her lips part for a moment and I see desire flash in her eyes. Then, Naomi swallows and her expression changes.

"This is probably inappropriate," she says, laughing nervously. "I'm half drunk, hugging my client. All the while my boss is inside for her bachelorette party. I could probably get fired."

"For talking to me?"

She chews her lip, staring at my face and letting her gaze drop down my body. Her look sends a thrill straight down my spine, and all I want to do is wrap my arms around her again, tilt her chin up towards me and taste those soft, pink lips of hers.

Finally, Naomi shakes her head. "Let's go back in. They're probably waiting for me."

"They're probably still drunkenly dancing and haven't even noticed you're gone."

Naomi grins, smacking my arm and shaking her head. I wrap my arms around her and she melts into me. It feels so good to have her near. My whole body is drawn to her like a magnet. She puts her hands on my chest and slowly pushes herself away. She bites her lip and the fire in my belly ignites.

I want her so fucking bad.

"You're trouble," she grins.

"Is that a bad thing?"

"Depends."

"On what?"

Instead of answering, she just shakes her head and laughs, turning back to the door. She looks over her shoulder, nodding towards the sound of the music.

"You coming?"

"I was thinking we might get out of here," I reply. Naomi's eyes widen and she turns towards me. I take a step closer to her, running my hand over her hip. She shivers, leaning towards me slightly. When she opens her eyes, she's got a sad smile on her face.

"I can't," she says, shaking her head. A sharp, burning pain passes through my chest. Naomi puts a hand on my chest and sighs. "We work together. It would be wrong. You're making such great progress with your knee, I don't want to do anything that might jeopardize that."

"Are you saying you care more about my knee than you do about me?" I ask, forcing a smile on my lips.

"I guess so, yeah. I am saying that," she laughs. She slides her hand to my shoulder and stands up on her tip toes. Her soft skin brushes mine as she lays a kiss on my cheek. She's so close it's making my head spin.

"Sorry I asked," I reply. "Maybe I've had too much to drink. I didn't mean to... you know. Proposition you or whatever. I've put you in an awkward situation."

"Under any other circumstances, I would have said yes."

My eyes widen as my whole body throbs for her.

I watch her turn back towards the door. The music gets loud and soft again as the door opens and closes behind her. I run my fingers through my hair, groaning.

That was the nicest rejection I've ever had, but it still stings. She's right, obviously. It would be a terrible idea to sleep together. I'd probably end up sabotaging the whole thing and have to find a new physical therapist right as my knee is starting to feel better.

But as much as I repeat that to myself, I can't forget the way her body feels in my arms, or how the heat in my veins ignites whenever her skin touches mine.

6
___

NAOMI

THE MUSIC HITS me like a wall as soon as I step inside. It takes a second for my eyes to adjust to the darkness, but I spot Ariana and Meg right away. They're at the bar. Ariana has some poor man hanging off her, as usual. She's laughing, but I can tell she's just flirting for the sake of flirting.

I make my way over to them, looking over my shoulder half-hoping to see Max. I wouldn't go home with him. At least, I don't think I would. But if he asked me again, it would be hard to resist.

I want him. I can't deny it. He's the sexiest man I've ever seen. When he held me in his arms, all I wanted to do was run my fingers up under his shirt and feel his skin under mine. I wanted to feel the rippling of his muscles under my hands, and feel the power of his body as he held me tight.

I've touched his body before, but only in a professional setting. What would it be like if we weren't in my physical therapy office? What if we were in his bed, or in my bed, or anywhere else, for that matter?

When he looked at me, I was dying for him to kiss me.

But he's my client.

We work together.

It would be wrong and unethical.

And plus, he's *Max Westbrook!* He's in the tabloids, for crying out loud! His family is like, the richest family in New York or something. They do some sort of big business importing and exporting for huge corporations.

What would he want with me?

He was probably just drinking, and I was the easiest girl for him to chase tonight.

"So?" Meg asks with a raised eyebrow. "Should we change that sash from 'Bride Tribe' to 'Bride-to-be?'"

My cheeks warm and I shake my head. I accept a drink that Ariana hands me.

"No," I say to Meg.

"But..."

"But nothing!" I laugh, sipping the drink. I grimace, looking at the amber liquid. "What is this?"

"Long island iced tea," Ariana says. "I asked the bartender to make them extra strong."

"Of course you did." I roll my eyes and taste the drink again. 'Strong' is an understatement.

"Stop stalling," Meg says. "What happened!"

"Nothing happened, really. We talked about marriage and how we didn't like the pressure to get married. Then I came back inside."

Sort of.

"Yeah, right. And Ariana was just discussing the geopolitical importance of the Middle East with her new friend." Meg side-eyes me, shaking her head. "So where is he? He didn't come back in with you."

"He had to leave."

"Oh my gosh, Naomi, stop lying," Meg laughs. "Did he come on to you? Did you kiss?"

Ariana raises her eyebrow. "He is *smoking* hot. Those eyes, my god!"

"It was fine. It was professional," I lie. Meg and Ariana just laugh. I sip my drink and say a silent thanks when Julia comes barging into our conversation. We're soon swept up in another wave of dancing and drinks and celebrating her upcoming wedding. Meg gives me a loaded look and I just shrug.

I'm not lying, nothing happened.

Technically.

Well, it didn't feel like nothing. The way he held me made my whole body vibrate. It felt like a whole lot more than nothing.

But on paper? Nothing happened. We didn't kiss, I rejected his advances. I was professional.

Ish.

Except the part where he invited me back to his place and I was dying to say yes. I can overlook that as a drunken slip-up.

The whole thing feels like the complete opposite of professional. I can't help scanning the room for him. My eyes keep drifting to the front door, hoping that I'll see his wide, muscular shoulders slipping through. He's at least a head taller than everyone else wherever he goes, and I imagine locking eyes with him across the crowd.

It doesn't happen, though.

He didn't follow me in, and he's not here waiting for me to change my mind.

A drunk man puts his hand on my hip and I elbow him away. He tries to rub up against me again on the dance floor, and Ariana brings her heel down on his foot. He yelps and hops away from us as Ariana shields me.

"Oops," she shrugs, making sure he's as far away as possible. "My foot slipped."

"Thanks," I laugh. "Why do guys think they can just rub their junk all over girls? It's gross."

"Just break their toes with your heels," Ariana grins. "I have a hundred percent success rate with that strategy."

I grin, scanning the crowd again for Max. Finally, I shake my head and turn back to my friends. I put my arm around Julia as she sings along to the song. She's off-key and off-time, but she's happier than I've ever been in my life.

For the thousandth time tonight, I wonder if marriage isn't so bad after all. Maybe promising to commit to someone for the rest of your life isn't a jail sentence for women. Maybe it really is a celebration of love.

Not that I've ever had the opportunity. I never let myself get close enough to men for marriage to even be a remote possibility.

Tonight is the perfect example. I probably lost any chance I had to hook up with Max. Even though I know it's for the best, I can't help but feel disappointed. Isn't that how relationships start? With the thrill of someone new, and thinking, 'maybe I should, maybe I shouldn't'? Why is my reaction always to lean towards 'shouldn't' instead of 'should'?

Ariana has another man hanging off her, Meg is dancing and singing with Julia, and I'm just scanning the room for any sign of the man that I just turned down.

I down the rest of the Long Island iced tea and put the glass down on a nearby table before heading towards Meg and Julia. I plaster a smile on my face and start singing along with them. I'm greeted with smiles and hugs and they start singing louder.

I may have lost my chance with Max tonight, but that doesn't mean it has to ruin my evening. A Beyoncé song comes on over the speakers and the bridal party erupts into excited shrieks. I laugh, glancing one last time at the door. Then, I shake my head and do my best to forget about Max Westbrook.

7

MAX

THE RINGING of my phone wakes me up. It's the ringtone I've set for my mother's number, and based on the headache gathering behind my forehead, there's no way I'm going to pick up that phone call.

I wasn't kidding last night when I told Naomi they were pressuring me to get married. It's been the number one topic of conversation for most of my adult life.

They thought I'd marry Farrah in college, but she left me as soon as she knew my football career was over. They pressured me to marry every single girl that I ever dated after that. Once, I agreed with them, and I ended up leaving the poor woman at the altar.

That was all over the tabloids, just like every other mistake I make. Even Naomi's heard of the last one. The guilt still makes my chest burn when I think about Heather. I shouldn't have done that to her, and I won't do it to anyone else.

So, no. I'm not going to field any questions about my love life at 7am on a Sunday morning. My parents can wait.

I click 'ignore' and roll over, shoving a pillow over my head.

I'm not sure if it's my headache and the stale taste of beer in my mouth, or if it's the memory of Naomi's gentle rejection last night, but the thought of doing anything except lying in bed seems particularly unappealing this morning.

My phone rings again—Mom's ringtone, *again*.

Ugh.

It only takes a second to put my phone on silent. I lay back and stare at the ceiling, spreading my arms out wide in my king-size bed.

The sheets smell fresh and the pillows are soft and downy, but my bed feels cold. Naomi felt perfect in my arms last night. Even just hugging her outside the bar was intimate. I wonder what she would feel like naked in bed beside me?

I could bury my nose in her hair and inhale the sweet scent of roses that clings to her. I could wrap my arms around her, sinking my fingers into her flesh and memorizing every curve of her body. She could press her chest against mine and brush those soft, pink lips across my skin.

Shivering, I put my hand to my forehead.

I will not give in to the temptation. I won't touch myself.

The last thing I want is to be going to my next physio appointment with a hard-on, remembering how I jerked off to the thought of my physical therapist. I struggled enough on Monday, I don't want to associate Naomi with pleasuring myself.

I won't do that to myself. Being near her is torture enough.

Swinging my legs over the side of the bed, I steady myself before standing up. My head feels like it's full of lead, and I didn't even drink that much. I must be getting old.

Maybe rejection worsens hangovers?

I stand on two shaky legs, ready to wince as the pain of a knee stiffened by sleep shoots through my leg. As I straighten, my jaw drops open slightly. There's no pain. I take a tentative step towards the bathroom, shocked at how easy my movements are.

My knee's progress with Naomi has eclipsed all the other physical therapy I've done before. I was an idiot to try to come on to her. She was right to turn me down. Maybe I should be like her and care more about my knee. I should care more about my knee than I do about my dick.

Still, I'm not used to it—rejection. I'm used to women falling all over me. I'm used to having them follow me around wherever I am, batting their eyelashes and running their hands over my arms.

What I'm *not* used to is diving into conversations about marriage being an institution designed to keep women in their place. I'm not used to having a bright, beautiful woman battle with desire and propriety and have propriety win out.

I avoid looking at myself in the mirror when I get up to take a piss. I keep the lights off and shuffle back to bed. I flop down on my back and check my phone.

Twelve missed calls, all from my mother.

I groan.

I don't want to call her back. I'm clearly hungover, and I'm not in the mood for the inevitable questions about my love life.

Still, something could be wrong.

Sighing, I tap my screen until my mother's name pops up, and let my finger hover over the 'call' button. With a deep breath, I press down and bring the phone to my ear.

She answers halfway through the first ring.

"Max! Finally!"

"Hey, Mom."

"I've been trying to get a hold of you forever!"

"It's not even eight AM, Mom, what's going on?"

"Well," she huffed. I could picture her smoothing her hair down and patting her cheeks in that perfect, rehearsed movement of hers. "Your father and I saw the papers this morning."

"Okay...". Am I supposed to know what that means?

"And we saw *you* in them," she continues.

"Uh-huh."

"We got the shock of our *lives*, didn't we, Rudy?" I imagine my father nodding in agreement.

Her little breadcrumb trail of hints is starting to frustrate me. I close my eyes and bring my hand to the bridge of my nose, willing myself to keep my voice patient.

"I haven't seen the papers, Mom," I answer. "What did they say?"

"Well!" She exclaims and I swallow back another wave of frustration. *Just spit it out!* "When were you going to tell us you had a girlfriend! You let us find out like the rest of the world. I've been getting phone calls from all the girls at the club all morning!"

'The girls at the club' is code for the gaggle of women who pretend to be friends from the Country Club. They have nothing better to do than gossip about me, apparently. And they'd been calling her all morning? About *my girlfriend?*

I try to process what my mother is saying, but nothing makes sense.

"Mom, I don't have a girlfriend."

"Max, first you keep us in the dark, and then you *lie* to me! I've seen the photos!"

"What photos?"

"In the paper!"

40

The exasperation bubbles up inside me and threatens to boil over. I sit up in bed, taking a long, calming breath.

"Mom, I'm not lying. What paper did you see these photos in?" I start walking towards my laptop.

"The Post."

"Oh my god, Mom," I sigh. "That's hardly where you get your news, is it?"

"Stop stalling, Max. When do we get to meet her?"

I fire up my laptop, tapping on the keyboard until I pull up the New York Post's website. I only have to scroll to the second news story to see my face.

My stomach drops.

It's my face... and Naomi's.

"So...???" My mom huffs on the other end of the line. "Your father and I are going to come to the city to meet her."

"Mom, no, I—"

"I need to go now, I'm getting another call. We'll be there shortly. I'll bring your grandmother's ring."

"*Mom!*"

The phone clicks and the line goes dead. I stare at my phone's screen, and then back at the computer. There are half a dozen photos of Naomi in my arms. Even if we're not kissing or embracing in any of them, we look... *intimate*. For once, I agree with my mom. If I'd seen these photos, I would think we were a couple.

Then, her final words finally sink in. *I'll bring your grandmother's ring.*

She thinks I'm going to *marry* Naomi!

My stomach tumbles and I try to dial my mom's phone again, but it's her turn to ignore my call. I find my dad's number and call him.

"Dad—" I say, breathless, as he answers.

"Max," he replies. "You spoke to your mother?"

"Yeah, about that. The girl in the photo, she's—"

"Max, listen to me." His voice is hard and I pause. My heart starts thumping. I only hear that tone in his voice when things were very, very wrong. "Your mother and I have been very patient with you. We saw you ruin not one, but *two* good relationships."

"Farrah wasn't—"

"*Two* good relationships," he continues. "And we're at the end of our rope. After the accident, I gave you a position at the company."

"Dad, I don't see what this—"

"It was with the understanding that you would make the family proud, and you would carry on the family name. Your mother and I are tired of reading about you gallivanting all over New York City. We're tired of the gossip, tired of the stories, tired of it all. It's not good for you and it's not good for the company."

Yeah, and you care more about the company than you do about me.

He pauses for dramatic effect, and it works. "So you have two choices right now."

I hold my breath.

"You can either marry that woman, or you can give up your position at the company and all the benefits that go with that. You'll no longer be part of this family. Not now, not in my will, nothing."

"What?"

"You heard me. We're sick of this. If this woman is suitable, then she's the one."

"She's the 'one'?! If she's 'suitable'? What the fuck?"

"Your bachelor lifestyle has gone on long enough. This has to end."

My eyes widen and I almost drop my phone. I just barely

hear him hang up. I'm glad I'm sitting at my desk, because my legs feel too weak to stand on.

I replay the two conversations I've just had with my parents over and over in my mind until I finally understand what's going on: I can either marry Naomi, or lose my job, my inheritance, and my family.

8

NAOMI

SUNDAY DINNERS at my mom's house are a tradition. I walk out my door just after noon, still feeling slightly groggy from last night. I drank more than I usually do, but mostly all I can think about is Max. I keep replaying our conversation over and over in my head. I still don't know if turning him down was the right decision.

Professionally? Absolutely.

Personally? I'm not so sure.

My mom lives halfway to Ithaca, in a little sleepy village on her own. She grows her own vegetables, and spends her days making art. So basically, she has the opposite life to mine. How I ended up at one of the busiest physical therapy practices in New York City is beyond me.

Maybe the sleepy little village was a little too sleepy for me.

It takes a couple hours to get there, so maybe the drive will clear my head. Maybe by the time I get there, I'll have forgotten about last night. About Max.

Ariana calls me as I'm heading out the door.

"How'd your night end up?"

"It was fine," I answer, pinning my phone between my shoulder and my ear as I lock my front door. "Got home about midnight."

"Party animal," she says sarcastically.

"That's me," I laugh.

"You still happy you turned down Mr. Westbrook?"

"Define 'happy'."

Ariana laughs.

"What about you?" I continue, heading down the steps towards the front door of my building. My car is parked on the street.

"Oh, I was home about three. I actually had a lot of fun! You wanna go out for a late lunch today?"

"Can't, heading to my mom's."

"Oh, right, Sunday. Will she be disappointed in you that you were celebrating someone's wedding?"

"She's not that bad," I laugh. "She just doesn't want *me* to get married."

"Too bad for Max."

"Stop it," I laugh. "Gotta go, just got to my car."

"Call me tonight, maybe we can meet up when you get back."

As soon as I say goodbye and hang up the phone, it rings again. I frown when I see the screen blinking with an unlisted number. Usually, I wouldn't answer phone calls from people I don't know, but something makes me move my thumb over the green circle.

"Hello?"

"Naomi! Hi. Hey. I, uh... it's Max."

"Max?" I frown. *Max Westbrook?* "How did you get my phone number?"

"You gave me your business card."

"Oh. Right." I lean against my car, frowning as I press the

46

phone into my ear. Why is Max calling me? Butterflies explode all over my stomach.

"Sorry to call you on a Sunday."

"That's all right, is everything okay with you knee?" I ask the question, hoping that he's not calling me about his knee. A part of me wants him to be calling me for *me*.

But that would be ridiculous... right?

"I'm not calling about my knee."

The butterflies go nuts. I open my car door and slip inside, closing myself in against the noise and the cold of the street.

"Oh."

"I was calling..." He trails off and I hear him sigh. "I'm calling..."

"Is everything okay?"

"Are you free right now? You want to meet for a coffee?"

"I..."

"I won't ask you to come back to my place, I promise."

I laugh despite myself. "Damn, I was hoping for a second chance." I blush as soon as the words come out of my mouth, and quickly cover it up by continuing: "I'm supposed to meet my mom, but I can probably spare an hour."

"Great, is there a coffee shop near you? Where is convenient for you?"

"Yes, there are coffee shops near me," I laugh. "This is New York City."

"Right." I can hear the grin in his voice.

"I'll send you the name of one nearby. Meet you there in fifteen?"

MY HEART THUMPS as I drive towards the coffee shop. Why

does Max want to meet? What could he possibly want to talk about?

Does he want to apologize for last night? Does he want to ask me out again?

Somehow, it seems more serious than that. His voice was strained. He seemed tense. He wasn't his usual confident self.

I consider calling Meg or Ariana, but I decide to hold off. I want to see what he says first. They'd probably just tease me and make me more nervous than I already am.

Parking the car, I check the time. I have about an hour before I need to leave for my mom's. That should be enough to hear him out... right?

I order a couple coffees and wait at a table by the window. It doesn't take long for Max to arrive. I see him pull up in a sleek black sports car, walking out as if he were a movie star.

I mean, he might as well be. His family is ultra-rich, and he's basically New York City's golden boy. Or New York City's favorite bad boy, whichever way you want to look at it. He closes the car door and I watch his biceps bulge with the movement. His clean white t-shirt stretches over his chiseled body, and I wonder for the thousandth time what he looks like unclothed.

He sees me right away and a smile breaks over his face. My heart flutters.

"I got you a regular black coffee, I don't know what your drink order is."

"Venti soy latte half foam half sweet extra hot, with whip" he rattles off as he slides into the chair.

"Oh, I..." really? *That's* his order?

"I'm joking," he laughs. "Black coffee *is* my drink order." His eyes sparkle as he grins, and my heart melts.

I laugh, shaking my head. "I was worried for a second."

48

"Why, can't handle a man with a complicated coffee order?"

"I don't think I can, no."

"That says a lot about you, I'm afraid."

"Call me old fashioned, but coffee is where I draw the line."

Max laughs, and his perfect smile sends spears of warmth through my body. I squeeze my legs together, swallowing a sip of coffee to cover my blush.

"So, what's up?" I ask when I've regained my composure.

Max's smile melts off his face and he stares out the window. His fingers play with the edge of his coffee cup, and his chest heaves as he takes a deep breath.

"First of all, I'm sorry about last night. I thought... I shouldn't have..."

"It's okay, Max. Under any other circumstances I would have been all over you."

His eyes swing back to mine and I see the desire darken them. I lick my lips, wondering if I should have said that. What is our next physical therapy appointment going to be like? Can I still be a professional after this? Even meeting him here is probably inappropriate.

His appointment is tomorrow. I'll be massaging his glutes, thinking about what he looks like naked.

Great.

Max leans his elbows on the table, staring at the space between us. Before I can stop myself, I reach over and put my hands over his. His skin is warm and smooth, and I can feel the strength of his broad hands underneath mine. He twists his fingers into mine and looks up at my face.

"I have a favor to ask of you."

"Okay..." I reply. My heart is thumping from the contact of

our hands. I'm not sure I can handle much more of his intense gaze without wetting my pants with desire.

Right now, I'd do anything he asks.

"There were photos of us in the papers."

"What?" I stiffen.

"In the Post. They saw us outside. I'm sorry."

"I... what kind of photos?"

"Nothing bad. They caught us hugging." He pulls his hand away and I yearn for the contact again. He reaches down and pulls out his phone, spinning it around to show me. My jaw drops as I take it from him.

"This says we're dating. I could be fired! *'Max Westbrook canoodles with mystery girl'?*" I look at him. "Canoodles?!"

"I know." He takes a deep breath. "I need—I would love —" He sighs. "It would help me out a lot if you pretended like we were engaged."

You could hear a pin drop. My jaw falls open, and my eyes widen.

"What?"

"I know it's crazy. I *know*. I'm not a psycho, I promise. It's just..." His eyes go up towards the ceiling and then he closes them, taking a deep breath.

"My parents saw the photos. They told me that they were coming to meet you, and if this turned out to be another girl that didn't matter, they would fire me from the company."

"*What?!*"

"I'll lose my job, my inheritance—everything. You don't have to pretend forever! I just need to buy a little time until I can figure something out, until I can talk some sense into them."

I stare at him, mouth agape.

"I'll pay you for your time. I'll talk to your boss. We can keep it quiet. I just..." His face crumples as his eyebrows draw together, and I already know I'm not going to be able to say no if I stay here much longer. "Please, Naomi. I'm desperate."

"Let me think about it."

He catches my hand before I can stand up, and drills his eyes into mine. "Naomi, I wouldn't ask if I didn't need it. If I lose my job... I'll lose everything. My family will cut me off and shut me out of their entire network. I'll have nothing. Those people—they're ruthless."

I can hear the desperation in his voice. I swallow, and squeeze his hand.

"I just need you to pretend to be my fiancée for a month, maybe two. That will give me enough time to figure out my next move. I'll give you a quarter million per month."

I freeze.

"*Two hundred and fifty thousand dollars?*"

"Per month."

"Let me think about it. I'll call you tonight, give me your number. Yours was unlisted."

Max nods, scratching his number on a napkin and handing it to me. "Tonight?"

"Tonight."

9

MAX

I watch Naomi get into her car and my heart squeezes. I drop my head into my hands and take a deep breath. I feel like I've made a mistake. I shouldn't have asked that of her. I shouldn't have put her in that position. She must think I'm completely crazy.

But what else can I do?

I just need time. My parents will be here tomorrow at the latest, and they'll want to know who the girl in the photo is. If I tell them she was just a girl I met at the bar, they'll cut me off. If I tell them the truth, that she's my physical therapist and that nothing is happening between us... well, they clearly didn't want to hear anything I had to say. And if they don't believe me, the consequences are too steep.

I can't give up my entire life, my job, my income for something like this. I've already lost everything once, I can't go through that again. I just need time to figure out my next move.

Naomi said she'd think about it, but what will she decide? I'll pay her, of course I will. I don't give a fuck about the money. But the way she looked at me... I don't want her to think less of me.

Between last night and today, it might be too late.

She told me that under different circumstances, she'd have been all over me. Even if that wasn't a joke, I'm pretty sure I've burned that bridge forever now. I might have to find a new physical therapist after all.

I grab the coffee cup and head out towards my car. It only takes a few minutes for me to get to Joel's house. He greets me in his boxers, with the face of someone who was out all night.

"Hey," he grunts. "You look like hell."

I chuckle. "You clearly haven't looked in the mirror, then."

"Fuck," he groans, collapsing onto the couch. His hand flies to his forehead. "What happened last night?"

"I left pretty early."

"With the physio? I saw you walk out with her."

"Nah."

Joel's eyes widen and he looks at me. "She turned you down?"

"It's not like that."

"Right." He coughs, clutching his stomach and groaning. "I'm never drinking again."

I get up and get two glasses of water. Joel accepts it gingerly before gulping half of it down.

"So what happened?"

Instead of answering, I pull out my phone. I get the photos on the Post's website up and turn the screen towards him. Joel frowns, staring at the pictures and trying to get his eyes to focus.

"What's this?"

"Fucking paparazzi."

"They're *still* after you? Why do they care about you?"

"Fuck if I know."

"So? What's the big deal."

"My parents have seen it."

Joe's mouth drops into a small 'oh', and he nods. "They think she's 'the One'?"

"They don't think that. They're sure of that. They're coming to the city tomorrow to meet her."

"What?!"

"Yeah."

"What are you going to do?"

I shrug, sighing. "I asked her to pretend."

Joel sits up, planting his hands on his knees. He leans forward, staring at me as if he's seeing me for the first time.

"You asked your physical therapist to pretend to be your fiancée so that your parents wouldn't freak out about you being in the papers with some random woman again?"

I chuckle. "That about sums it up, yeah."

"You're a fucking lunatic."

"Apple, tree, you know how it goes. They said they'd cut me off if I didn't take this seriously."

Joel leans back, staring at the wall in front of him. "So what did she say?"

"Who?"

He rolls his eyes, looking at me like I'm denser than lead. "The physio, dickhead. What did she say when you proposed to her?"

"Her name is Naomi."

Joel takes another sigh, staring up at the ceiling as if he's praying for patience. "Fine. Well what did *Naomi* say when you *fucking proposed to her.*"

I'm kind of enjoying pushing his buttons. I know he just wants the best for me, and he's being a good friend, but my head is a mess and seeing Joel get frustrated over something simple is the most entertainment I've had all day.

"She said she'd think about it."

"What does that mean?"

"I don't know."

We're silent for a while. Joel groans as he pushes himself up, reappearing with two cans of beer. He hands me one, grinning.

"I didn't shake this one up, I promise."

"What happened to 'never drinking again'?"

"I reconsidered."

I glance at my watch. "I guess it's after twelve, so we can drink now."

"I don't care what time it is, I need a drink to take the edge off this hangover."

"You know all that does is prolong the hangover, right?"

Instead of answering, he just cracks open the beer. I chuckle and do the same. When the cold beer hits my tongue, I close my eyes and lean back.

"So," Joel starts. "Basically, you're fucked. You have to pretend to be engaged to Naomi in order to keep your job and your inheritance. When and if your parents find out that the engagement is all fake, they'll cut you off anyway." He holds up the beer. "Your fake engagement is just like having a beer to cure a hangover."

"Or, they'll never find out."

"What's your end game, here? Leave her at the altar?"

Ouch.

"Look, your past with women hasn't exactly been perfect either."

"We're not talking about me right now," Joel grins. "I'm not trying to be a dick here. I know why you asked her. But it just seems like maybe it would be a better idea to just *talk* to your parents?"

"Have you *met* my parents?"

Joel laughs. "Fair point," he says. "They're almost as bad as mine."

"The 'girls from the club' were calling my mom all morning."

Joel groans. "My mom was probably the first one on the phone to her."

"It's a miracle we turned out normal."

"Are we normal?" Joel laughs. "You're considering fake-marrying your physio just so your parents don't cut you out of your inheritance and job. That doesn't exactly seem normal."

"Shut up, Joel."

Joel just laughs and fumbles for the remote. He flicks the TV on and finds the sports channel. "Football's about to start. Text Connor and Graham, tell them to bring some food."

"Alright."

For now, at least, I can think about football and I can forget about Naomi, my parents, weddings—all of it. Or at least, I *think* I can forget about it, until my college ex-girl-friend's face pops up on the screen.

"*And newly engaged couple, Farrah Harris and the New York Giants Quarterback, Elijah Matthews. Congratulations to the happy couple.*"

I groan. Joel glances at me, then back at the screen.

"Well, at least she got the husband she wanted," I say bitterly.

"What a fucking gold digger," Joel spits. He was there when she left me the day after my injury, and he saw her chase after the next star quarterback. Looks like she's made it all the way to the top. I reach down towards my knee, massaging the sore tissue as I stare at her smiling face.

It feels like she's smiling at me, spiting me through the television.

Joel reaches over and puts a hand on my shoulder.

"Look at the bright side, Max. At least you're engaged now, too."

I punch his arm and he yelps as he laughs, throwing his hands up. I can't help but grin with him, and I breathe a sigh of relief when Farrah's face disappears from the screen.

This week, I just can't get away from weddings, engagements, women, and heartbreak.

10

NAOMI

THE DRIVE to my mom's house is a blur. It's a good thing I've travelled this route hundreds of times, because I don't remember any part of my drive here. When I pull in to her driveway, I turn off the car and rest my head on the top of the steering wheel. I take a deep breath to try to clear my head.

Max's words are still swirling around my head.

He wants to *marry* me?

I mean, he doesn't really want to marry me. He wants to tell his parents that he's marrying me, which isn't the same thing. Does that sting? Am I offended by that?

I don't even know how I feel.

My mom's house is small and tidy, and it looks exactly the same as last week. Or does it?

For the first time, I notice the paint peeling on the side of the house. The roof looks worn, and the planters aren't bursting with plants like they used to. I get out of my car and take a deep breath of fresh, country air before heading up the flagstones towards the front door.

I pull my jacket tighter around me, crossing my arms and

burying my chin into my chest. Winter is definitely on its way.

There are weeds poking up between the stones which makes me frown. Usually, Mom would have her garden looking immaculate, even in the fall.

When I get to the front door, something doesn't feel right. It's like I'm seeing the house for the first time—the worn paint, the creaky steps, the weeds. I look in the mailbox and pull out a stack of letters.

My heart drops when I flick through them. A big, red stamp with the word 'FORECLOSURE NOTICE' is plastered across one of the letters. My eyes widen, and the blood starts pumping in my ears.

"Mom?"

I knock on the door before opening it, calling out again as I step through.

"In here, honey!" My mom calls from the kitchen. The smell of warm, home cooking wafts through the familiar hallways as I make my way towards the back of the house.

"Hey, Mom," I say as I lay a kiss on her cheek. She's wearing a white apron with little yellow flowers on it, using an old wooden spoon to stir a pot of pasta sauce.

"Hi, honey," she says with a smile. "You're here later than usual this week."

"I had to make a stop on the way," I say vaguely, dropping the stack of mail on the kitchen table.

"Oh yeah?" She says, poking her head in the fridge.

"Hey, Mom," I say, picking up the foreclosure letter. "What's this about?"

Her long, grey-streaked hair is tied back in a braid down her back. She turns towards me, looking over her glasses towards me. Her lips pinch together and she straightens up, grabbing the letter and stuffing it in her apron pocket.

"Mom," I start.

"It's nothing."

"What's going on?"

"Everything is fine, honey. Don't worry about a thing. Dinner's ready, will you grab the plates?"

"Mom, I'm not letting this go."

My mother turns her back to me and leans her hands on the counter, dropping her head to her chest. Her shoulders look slight as she takes a deep breath. She turns to me slowly, wringing her hands and staring at the ground. She takes another deep breath, finally dragging her eyes back up to mine.

"I missed a couple payments."

"Why? Do you need money? I can help you, Mom."

She shakes her head. Her eyes fill with tears.

"I have breast cancer."

My stomach drops. The room spins. I stumble backwards, grabbing for a chair and sinking into it. My mother comes to me, wrapping her arms around my head and hushing me, cooing and making comforting noises as she strokes my hair.

"It's okay, Naomi. It's okay, shh," she says.

"You shouldn't be comforting me, Mom," I say, pulling away. "Why didn't you tell me?"

"Oh, I didn't want you to worry, Naomi. I know that you worry, and I didn't want to say anything until I knew more."

"And the foreclosure...?"

She takes a deep breath, sitting down in the chair next to mine and putting her hand over mine. Just like the house, it's like I'm seeing her for the first time. Her skin is papery-thin, and her face is drawn. Her green eyes don't seem as bright as they used to be. They're almost yellow. She looks so, so tired.

"I remortgaged the house to pay for the treatments," she explains. "I had to get rid of my health insurance, you know.

And business has been slow lately, so I haven't been able to pay the bank back."

If my mother is saying 'business is slow', that means business is non-existent. I grew up watching her paint huge canvasses, selling her work and sustaining us with her art.

But these days, people just don't seem to be buying paintings anymore. I've watched her do odd jobs to make ends meet, always being resourceful, and always refusing my help.

"Mom," I say, as my heart breaks. Tears gather in my eyes, spilling over onto my cheeks. My mom's eyes mist up and she brushes her frail thumb across my cheek.

"Don't worry, honey, it'll all be fine."

"How do you know that?"

She sighs, looking over at the pot of bubbling sauce. She heaves herself up and walks over to the pot, stirring it slowly.

"Grab some plates, Naomi. Let's eat."

We put everything aside and eat together. I tell her about work, avoiding anything relating to Max Westbrook. I focus on her, checking that she has enough groceries and supplies for the week. My heart breaks every time I see her labored movements, and I hold back all the comments and questions that flood through me.

By the time dinner is over, she hugs me again with the strength that only a mother has. She kisses my cheek and looks into my eyes.

"Don't worry about me, Naomi."

"Let me help you, Mom. I don't want to lose the house."

She takes a deep, shuddering breath, nodding her chin down slightly. "Thank you, Mimi."

With another hug, she lets me go. I climb back into my car, watching her silhouette wave at me in the doorway. She closes the door and I turn on the car. I only make it around the corner when I have to pull over. I break down. The tears flow down my cheeks and drip off my chin until my pants are soaked and I'm a blubbering, sniffling mess. I get a little packet of tissues out of my bag and clean myself up, and then take my phone in trembling hands.

I find the napkin with Max's number on it, and type it in to my phone. As soon as I send the message, I know that my life is going to change forever. Three little words that will shape my future:

I'll do it.

11

MAX

I PACE back and forth across my living room, checking the time for the thousandth time. She said she'd come here when she got back to the city, but it's almost ten o'clock at night and she's not here yet. How long does dinner with her mom usually take?!

This is a mistake.

I shouldn't be putting her in this position. I should just man up and talk to my parents. They shouldn't be forcing a wife on me, anyways!

I slump down on the couch and drop my head in my hands. A bead of sweat runs down the back of my neck, and my heart feels like it's beating erratically. I massage my temples, keeping my eyes closed as I take deep breaths through my nose.

I've gone around in circles ever since my parents called this morning. I don't have a choice. I've heard that tone in my father's voice before, and he never backs down from it.

He was serious when he said he'd cut me off and fire me if I kept up my lifestyle. But that shouldn't mean I have to marry a woman I'm not even dating! We were just in a picture together, nothing more.

I blow the air out of my nose and stare at the ceiling. This is the only way. I just need to make it through this visit from them, and then I can make up some story about Naomi and I parting ways. That will buy me enough time to figure out how to handle my parents.

A knock on the door makes me jump. I stand up, my bare feet sinking into the thick rug for a moment as I stare at the door.

This is it.

My heart is hammering and my mouth is suddenly dry. Even though this is insane, even though this is a ridiculous situation to be in, there's a part of me that's excited to see Naomi.

She's *here*.

I get to talk to her without the stark fluorescent lights of the physio office beaming down on us, without the thumping music from the bar beside us, without prying eyes and flashing cameras.

Just her, and me.

My palms are sweaty, so I wipe them on my jeans as I walk to the door. Taking a deep breath, I put my hand on the doorknob and turn.

"Hey," she says.

My heart drops to my stomach. Naomi's eyes are shining with tears, and her skin, typically smooth as porcelain, is blotchy and red. Her hands are clasped in front of her as if she's trying to stop them from trembling.

This isn't what I wanted. A lump forms in my throat and I struggle to swallow past it.

"Hey," I croak.

"Can I come in?"

I step aside, closing the door behind her. She kicks off her shoes before I can tell her to keep them on, lining them up against the wall next to the front door. Her eyes sweep across my apartment and I see a slight lifting of her eyebrows.

"Nice place."

"Thanks. Beer?"

"Sure."

We don't speak while I go to the fridge. She takes a seat at the kitchen island, accepting the green bottle of beer with a nod. She takes a sip, closing her eyes and drinking as if she needs the liquid courage.

My heart squeezes.

This isn't what I intended.

"Look, Naomi," I start. "I think this was a mistake. You... I don't want to put you in this position."

"In what position?"

I open my mouth and close it again, leaning against the counter across from her. Taking a deep breath, I choose my words carefully.

"You don't seem like you want this. To... to marry me. Or pretend to marry me, I mean."

"Tell me about your parents," she replies suddenly. "Why did you ask me to do this? Why can't you just talk to them?"

We stare at each other for a moment, and a bitter snort escapes me. I shake my head.

"Where do I start?"

"At the beginning."

I grin, nodding my head towards the couch in the living room. She follows me, and I sit down on one end of the three-seater while she sits at the far end, tucking one leg underneath her and resting her chin on her other knee. She's curled herself into a tiny ball, with her long, red hair falling like a curtain over her shoulder.

Even with a bright red nose and sadness in her eyes, she's still the most beautiful woman I've ever seen. All I want to do is reach over and wrap my arms around her. I want her to tell me why she's so sad, why she decided to accept my proposal. I want to know what she's thinking and what she's scared of.

But I can't ask her anything. She's staring at me, waiting for me to speak. So I do what she said: I start at the beginning.

"My parents started a company when they were in their twenties. My mother borrowed a bunch of money from her father, who ran an import-export business, and my father was a clever, ambitious young man. They built the company up to what it is now. They supply all kinds of materials for huge construction projects on the entire eastern seaboard."

I take a sip of my beer, glancing over at Naomi. Her eyes are glued on my face, as if she's listening to the things I'm saying and the things I'm not saying, all at once.

"I'm an only child. I found out a couple years ago that my mom miscarried a bunch of times, and finally they had me when they were almost forty. I was their golden child."

"I'm an only child, too," Naomi says softly. I look at her, nodding. "Sorry," she continues. "Go on."

"Well, they handed me the world. I went to the best schools. They wanted me to study business and come and work for them. They wanted me to get married and do what they had done—make something of myself and become the next generation of Westbrook 'power couples'. But then, I fell in love with football. To their credit, my parents embraced it. Maybe they saw it as an opportunity to be a different kind of 'power couple'. I had the best coaches, trainers—everything. By the time I went to college, I was already being scouted by NFL teams."

I take another sip of beer, trying to ignore the pang in my chest.

"Then your knee happened," Naomi finishes for me.

I nod, not wanting to meet her eye. If I look at her, the mist in my eyes might turn to real tears. "My knee happened. I was dating this girl, and she left me the next day, as soon as the doctor told me I'd never play football again."

"Max..."

I shake my head, swallowing past the lump that's reappeared in my throat.

"It's fine. I graduated, my parents gave me a good job, and now I'm working my way up their company. I have everything. They've given me everything."

"Have you told them you don't want to get married?"

I snort. "Yeah, I've told them. They don't get it. All they see is their society, where the women have their own power circles and the men have theirs. Single people don't make it."

I turn and look at Naomi again. She's unfolded her legs and is leaning against the couch's arm, resting her cheek against her closed fist. Her other hand is playing with the beer label, and she's staring out the windows at the twinkling lights of the New York skyline.

"So why'd you say yes?" I ask. "Last night, you said you didn't believe in marriage."

Naomi flinches, as if my words hurt her physically. My heart squeezes.

She takes a deep breath and then shrugs. "I got some bad news, and two hundred and fifty grand would solve a lot of problems."

She looks at me and I see the depth of pain in her eyes. I want to go to her, to wrap my arms around her and bury my nose in her hair. I want to kiss her forehead and rub her spine and tell her it'll all be okay. I want to give her as much money as she needs to fix whatever problems she has.

But I don't do any of that. I just nod.

"Okay," I say.

Naomi relaxes, as if she was worried I would pry. A small smile appears on her face, and she starts chuckling. She shakes her head, laughing a little bit harder.

"What?" I say, chuckling confusedly.

"I don't know," she laughs. "This is so ridiculous."

I grin. "I know."

She laughs, brushing her hair over her shoulder and shaking her head some more. She scratches the back of her head and looks out the window, deep in thought. She takes a long drink of beer, and then turns to me, pointing the bottle towards me.

"But I'm not going to sleep with you just because we're engaged. That's where I draw the line. That would be too complicated."

I grin. "Deal. You might have to kiss me in public to make it convincing, though."

A blush spreads over her cheeks, and heat blooms between my legs. Fuck, she's gorgeous. She turns towards me, scooting closer on the couch.

I move closer to her as well, until there's only a foot of space between us. She turns towards me, leaning forward and crawling her fingers towards me. She licks her lips and my heart thumps. Her eyes are shining with something, and I can't think about anything except how good it would feel to kiss her.

I lean towards her, my heart hammering against my ribcage. I smell the sweet floral scent that follows her everywhere, and feel the heat of her body. Her face is just inches from mine, and my heart is beating so fast that I think it might explode.

We're only inches apart, and I can feel her soft breath washing over my skin. Her eyes are wide and bright, and her lips are so fucking inviting.

This is what I've been dreaming of. This is the exact moment that I've been hoping for for almost a week. I inch closer, and then—

Knock! Knock! Knock!

We jump apart at the sound of banging on the door.

"Max! Open up!" My mother's voice floats through the closed door, and Naomi's eyes widen. My stomach drops as I jump to my feet.

"Who is that?!" Naomi hisses, staring at the door.

I take a deep breath, following her gaze. "That is my mother."

12

NAOMI

"Your mother is *here?!*" I whisper as my eyes widen. I glance towards the door again and back at Max. "Why is your mother here?"

"*Max, open up!*" A gruff voice comes through the door.

"And your father is here too?!"

"Oh my god," Max says, running his hands through his dark hair. He blows air out of his mouth as concern etches all over his face. "I'm so sorry. They said they were coming to the city, I didn't think they meant today."

"Are you fucking kidding me?!"

"I'm so sorry."

I would laugh if I wasn't so mortified. I look down at my grey tee-shirt and ripped jeans. I'm not wearing any makeup, and I know my hair could use a brush.

And now, I have to meet one of the richest couples in New York City, and I have to pretend to be engaged to their son?

I thought my day was bad before. I woke up with a hangover, and then got Max's bizarre proposal. When my mom told me that she had breast cancer, I thought that was as bad as it got.

I was wrong.

It just got worse. I watch Max rub his hands over his face. His forearms ripple with tension as he combs his hair back through his fingers, staring at the door as if he was afraid of what was on the other side.

I stand up and put my hands on his biceps, feeling the hard muscle under his skin as he drops his hands.

"I'm sorry," he whispers. "I had no idea."

"It's okay," I lie, forcing myself to smile. "Do I look okay?"

His eyes soften and he tucks a strand of hair behind my ear. "You look perfect."

My heart squeezes and I swallow. I don't know what all these emotions are. I don't know how to deal with the alternating waves of desire and fear and nervousness that attack me every time I take a breath. All I can do is just follow Max towards the door, wringing my hands in front of me as he turns the doorknob.

"Hey, Mom," he says and leans down to lay a kiss on her cheek. When he stands back up, I get the first glimpse of my soon-to-be fake mother-in-law.

She looks like a Stepford Wife mixed with a First Lady. Her hair is dyed a sandy blonde color, tied back in an ultra-neat bun at the base of her neck. She's wearing a perfectly pressed navy pantsuit, with an expensive-looking bag slung over her forearm. Her hands are manicured, with an array of sparkling rings displayed on her digits.

But it's her face that draws my attention. She has Max's eyes—bright and blue and deep and unreadable. They're focused on me, inspecting every inch of me as she steps through the door. Her heels click on the hardwood floor as she opens her arms towards me. She takes my hands in hers, squeezing them gently as she holds them out, blatantly looking me up and down.

"I'm sorry to barge in like this," she says, not looking sorry at all. "Aren't you going to introduce us, Max?"

Max shuffles to my side, putting an arm around my shoulders. Thankfully, his mother releases me and I put my arm around his waist. It feels stiff and uncomfortable. I can't imagine we look like a happy couple.

"Mom, Dad, this is Naomi. Naomi, this is my mom, Carol, and my dad, Rudy."

"Nice to meet you," I croak.

"Lovely to meet you, dear," Carol croons. Her eyes are still watching me like a hawk, and Max's hand tightens across my shoulders.

I try to speak, but nothing comes out. I clear my throat and nod to the kitchen. "Can I get you anything? Water? Beer? Coffee?"

"Coffee sounds good," Rudy says, shuffling towards the living room after he shakes my hand. "Thanks, Naomi."

I breathe a sigh of relief when I watch them walk towards the couch. That relief quickly turns to panic when I enter the kitchen.

I don't know where anything is!

I'm supposed to be marrying Max, and I have no idea how to make coffee at his house. Where are the filters? Where are the coffee grounds? Where are the mugs?

Where is the freaking coffee machine?! He'd better not have one of those stupid percolators. I don't think I can handle that right now.

My heart starts hammering in my chest as I glance around. I breathe a sigh of relief when I see his coffee machine with a little basket of pods next to it—single serving coffee. At least I won't have to worry about filters and coffee grounds.

I look through the basket and then call to them over my

shoulder. "You guys want 'Intenso', 'Luongo Forte' or, uh, decaf?" *Why don't these pods have normal freaking names?!*

"I'll have decaf, dear," his mother says, watching me from the couch. "And Rudy will have the same."

"Max?" Should I be calling him babe? Honey? Baby? I barely even know the guy! Am I being weird right now? Can they see how much I'm panicking? I turn towards them and wince when my hip hits the marble countertop of the island. I force a smile, and I'm pretty sure it just looks like my face is contorting weirdly.

"I'm good," Max says, shuffling some magazines and tidying a blanket that was strewn across the couch. He looks as stressed as I feel.

"Okay," I say under my breath. Now for mugs. Logically, they would be right above the coffee machine.

Nope.

Maybe the next cupboard over?

Nope.

I cough, trying to clear the lump in my throat as I open a third cupboard.

Still nothing.

I can feel Max's mom's eyes on my back. My heart is hammering. Where is Max? Why isn't he helping me? I never knew making a cup of coffee could induce so much panic. I'm looking through every single cupboard in this godforsaken kitchen looking for a mug to make coffee for my fake fiancé's mother, and she'll figure out that I've never been here before, and the whole gig will be up.

We won't pretend to be engaged, I won't get any money, and I won't be able to pay for my mom's treatment.

All because the stupid freaking mugs aren't where they are supposed to be, which is above the freaking coffee machine. What kind of monster stores the mugs on the other end of the kitchen?! I would never marry someone like that.

This is a disaster.

Finally, I open a wide drawer under the coffee machine and see the mugs neatly lined up. I sigh so loudly, I'm pretty sure they all hear me.

"Having trouble finding something?" Carol says. I glance over and see her eyebrow arched over her piercing blue eyes.

I laugh nervously. "I always do that. My kitchen at home has the mugs up top." I gesture awkwardly to the cabinets as a blush spreads from my cheeks to my neck. I scratch the back of my head, trying to smile.

"Ah," she says, nodding. Her eyes don't leave me. Max mouths 'sorry', and comes towards me.

With him beside me, I start to relax. He puts his hand on the small of my back and shows me how to work the machine.

"Everything will be fine," he whispers in my ear. "Thank you for doing this."

"I think the price just went up to three hundred grand. It's the price for surprise visits from in-laws. I need at least 48 hours notice from now on."

The corner of his lip twitches, and his chin dips down. "That seems fair," he chuckles. The machine rumbles to life and black coffee starts spluttering into the cup. I take a deep breath.

Max leans over and kisses my temple, sliding his hand over to my hip and pulling me into him. I close my eyes for a moment, inhaling his scent and letting the comfort of his touch wash over me.

"I'll get rid of them as soon as I can," he whispers as we make another cup of coffee.

I nod. It can't be soon enough.

13

MAX

"So, how did you two meet?" My dad asks, sipping his decaf coffee. I glance at Naomi and try to smile. In a perfect world, we would have come up with a story and rehearsed it. I would have prepared her. I would have told her about my parents—what to expect, what to say, what not to say.

But now?

None of that. I can't give her any warning. She looks like a deer in headlights, but she's doing fairly well.

So, when my dad asks me where we met, I just tell the truth.

"Naomi is my physical therapist," I explain. "I started going to her a few months ago, and I guess we just sort of clicked."

"How does your boss feel about the relationship?" He says, turning to Naomi.

Naomi shrugs, smiling. "She was surprised, but she's okay with it."

There's an awkward silence and I clear my throat.

"I wasn't expecting you guys here so soon."

"Well, we had to meet the woman who stole our son's

heart," my mother says, turning her hawk-like eyes towards Naomi. I wish she wouldn't do that. I reach over and put my hand on Naomi's knee, feeling her tremble slightly. She must be so stressed.

Hell, *I'm* stressed, and I'm their son!

"I'm not used to the whole tabloid thing," Naomi says. "That was a bit of a shock this morning."

My mother waves a hand and leans back in her chair. "You'll get used to it. If you lead a boring-enough life, they'll leave you alone."

"They haven't left Max alone," Naomi grins. "Maybe your life will finally be boring enough now."

"It doesn't feel boring," I reply. Naomi's eyes flash, and her grin widens. My shoulders relax slightly and I squeeze the hand on her thigh. She interlaces her fingers in mine, leaning back on the couch.

"How was the drive?" Naomi asks, and then frowns. "You... you drove here, right?" She tenses.

"Yes, of course, honey," my mother says. "How else would we get here? There are hardly any flights from Sands Point to the city. Well," she muses, staring out the window. "I guess you could take a sea plane." She looks at Naomi again, smiling that thousand-megawatt smile of hers. "The drive was fine. We missed the traffic, so it was all smooth sailing. We've been meaning to come to the city for a while now, so this was the perfect opportunity."

"Right."

There's a tense moment, and then my father starts asking me about work. I relax as we start talking about familiar, neutral territory, and Naomi's tenseness dissipates. She leans into me, squeezing my hand.

Is it bad that I like this?

As awkward and horrifying as it was to have my parents

walk in, I actually like sitting here, holding her hand. It feels almost natural.

Well, as natural as it could feel, under the circumstances.

After an hour of idle chit-chat, Naomi takes a deep breath.

"It's been lovely to meet you, but I have to work early tomorrow morning. I'm going to have to leave you guys to catch up without me."

Smooth.

She shoots me a glance as if to say, 'you're on your own', and I can't help but grin.

My father gets the hint, though, and he stands up. "We'll be on our way, won't we, Carol."

"Of course."

"Rudy, Carol," Naomi says, giving them both a kiss. We say our goodbyes, leading them back through the front door. As soon as the door closes, Naomi turns to me with wide eyes.

"You *bastard*," she says. "That was my worst nightmare!"

She's laughing now, and I can't help but join in. She leans against the kitchen counter, putting her hand against her forehead and laughing while she shakes her head. We laugh, leaning against the kitchen counter and letting out all the stress of the past hour. Tears are streaming down her face, and her emerald eyes are shining more than I've ever seen them.

I push myself off the counter and stand in front of her. I put my hands on her hips and pull her towards me, sinking my fingertips into her body and shaking my head.

"I'm so, so sorry about that. I was as shocked as you were."

"That's the only reason I'm still here," she laughs. "I could tell it was as hard for you as it was for me."

She puts her hands on my chest, curling her fingers into my shirt. My heart is racing. She's so close.

"You were perfect," I say. "They liked you."

"I felt like a blundering idiot," she says, shaking her head. "The mugs…"

"Don't worry about the mugs," I say in a hoarse whisper. She runs her fingers up to my shoulders, hooking her hands around my neck. I press my chest against hers, growling softly as I feel her body fitting into mine.

She stares at me and her eyes flick down to my lips. The fire in my stomach ignites, and my cock throbs between my legs.

Maybe it's the stress of the day, or the tension of the evening with my parents. Maybe it's the fact that Naomi has obviously had a stressful day, too.

Or, maybe it's just that I'm holding a beautiful woman in my arms, and she's looking at me with those bright, green eyes of hers and licking those perfectly kissable lips.

Whatever it is, my body feels like it's on fire. I'm so tightly strung I feel like I could explode at any moment. Neither of us move. Her chest is pressed against mine, her fingers hooking into the nape of my neck. She twists her fingers into my hair, tilting her head to the side.

I wrap my arms around her, letting them drift down to her ass. I pull her into me and I can't wait any longer. I dip my chin down and crush my mouth against hers. She parts her lips and kisses me fiercely, pulling me into her and gasping softly into my mouth as we melt into each other.

My whole body sings. My hands drift up her spine as she tangles hers into my hair. She kisses me, sliding her tongue into my mouth and moaning. Her lips taste like heaven.

This is more than a kiss. It's more than a stress relief.

This is pure passion. It's pure *want*. Pure longing.

Kissing Naomi feels better than I could ever have imagined, and when she pulls away from me, all I want to do is crush my lips against hers again.

My chest is heaving, and I rest my forehead against hers. We stay like that, eyes closed, holding each other, until Naomi lets out a single sigh.

"Wow," she says. "You're a good kisser."

14

NAOMI

THIS IS TOO MUCH.

I don't know what's happening, or why I'm doing this, but it's too much. My body is screaming at me to just strip down naked right here and wrap my legs around Max's muscular frame. Every nerve ending is begging for release. There's a ball of fire in the pit of my stomach, and my panties are completely soaked through.

That was more than a kiss.

It was incredible. It was an explosion of tension and passion and lust all rolled into one.

Even the way he's holding me now, cradling me against him as he rests his forehead against mine. He runs his finger along my jaw and tangles his fingers into my hair, and I melt into him again. I tilt my chin up and taste his lips.

We kiss more slowly this time, feeling each other more fully than the first time. I inhale the smell of his skin, wrapping my arms around his neck as I melt into his kiss. His hand drifts down my side, brushing my breast and coming to rest on my hip.

Every touch makes my whole body tremble.

I want him.

I want him more than I've wanted any other man.

And yet, when we pull apart, I take a deep breath. I don't think I can do this right now.

There's too much going on—too much between us. If I sleep with him now, what does that mean for us, for this engagement, for the money? For my mother?

Sex is complicated.

My whole body is screaming for it, and most of my mind wants it too.

But still, I take a deep breath and put a hand on his chest. He pauses, staring into my eyes as I shiver. I shake my head.

"I should go."

"You don't have to."

"I know, but I should."

Max nods.

"You're probably right."

"Probably."

It only takes a minute to gather my things. I sling my bag over my shoulder and hold it close as I look up at him. He has a hint of stubble across his jaw, and his hair is completely disheveled. His eyes are bright, and his lips are still glistening from our kiss.

He looks so perfectly kissable right now.

I bite my lip.

"So..."

"I'll call you tomorrow," he says. "We probably need to figure out the details of this..." he waves his hand. "Whatever this is. This engagement."

"Okay," I reply. No turning back now.

"I'll cancel my physio appointment for tomorrow. I have some paperwork to figure out, and I don't want to put you in an uncomfortable position. Maybe I can take you out to dinner?"

I nod. "Sure."

He leans down and kisses me again. It's soft, and tender. It's *intimate*, even though it only lasts a second. His hand lingers on my cheek, his face just next to mine.

"I won't do that if you don't want me to."

"It's okay," I reply, brushing my hand against his. "I'll talk to you tomorrow."

By the time I get to my car, my hands are shaking. I slide into the driver's seat and close my eyes. I gulp down air as if I've been drowning and my head has just broken the surface. It takes a few minutes for me to regain my composure. I put my hands on the steering wheel, and I take another deep breath.

With my hands still shaking, I dial Ariana.

"Hey," I say when she answers.

"Hey, girl," she says. "You okay?"

"I think so. Can I come over?"

"Of course. Meg is here, too."

"Perfect."

"You want us to get the wine ready?"

"It's like you read my mind," I laugh. "I'll be there in half an hour."

When I hang up, I feel calmer already. The girls will be able to ground me. If I tell them what's going on, they'll be able to let me know if I'm being absolutely crazy or not.

Too much has happened today. From Max's first proposal —if you can call it that—to finding out about my mom's cancer and the foreclosure on the house, and then to dealing with Max's parents... I just need some time with people that I trust, people that have been there for me.

I practically run up the steps to Ariana's apartment, and

she opens the door with her arms wide open. Meg isn't far behind with a glass of wine in one hand and a pint of Ben and Jerry's in the other. Before I know it, tears are streaming down my face. They don't ask me anything, they don't say anything, they just sit me down and fill me with wine and ice cream and laughter.

"Naomi," Ariana starts. "I have to tell you about last night. I ended up going home with this guy Rolf."

"Rolf?"

"Literally Rolf. R-O-L-F. I made him show me his ID because I didn't believe that was his name. He was Swedish and he looked like the guy from True Blood."

I laugh. "Hot."

"To look at, yeah, he was perfect. I couldn't understand anything he was saying, though," Ariana laughs. "But you know, he got the job done." She winks and I laugh some more. My shoulders relax a little and I take a sip of wine.

"Were you still at the bar when Julia was dancing on the table?" Meg asks, dumping a bag of chips into a bowl.

"No, when was that?!"

"Must have been one in the morning, or something. She fell off and smashed one of the chairs. That's why we got thrown out."

"You got thrown out?!" That makes me laugh so hard I get a stitch in my side. Tears are streaming down my face, but this time I don't mind. My heart feels light. We lean against each other, laughing and eating and drinking until Ariana puts her hand on my leg and looks me in the eye.

"So what's up, Naomi? How's your mom?"

My lip trembles and my chest squeezes, and I can't even get a single word out. Meg scoots closer and puts her arm around my shoulder.

"Just tell us when you're ready," she says softly. "Shh. Tell us when you're ready."

I make a weird snorting, sniffling, hiccupping sound as I try to talk just as a huge sob racks my body, and then I try to laugh and another weird snorting sound comes out of me.

Ariana laughs, grabbing a box of tissues and handing them to me. "That bad, huh?"

"I don't even know where to start."

I look at my friends as the tears fill my eyes, and they just hug me until I'm able to talk.

15

MAX

I PARK my car outside her office and glance at the clock. I'm early—Naomi won't be done with work for another fifteen minutes. I check my hair in the rear view mirror, smoothing my eyebrows and making sure my breath is okay. I pop a mint in my mouth just for good measure.

I don't even know what I'm expecting. My whole body has been on edge ever since we kissed. My shirt collar is rubbing against the back of my neck, and I adjust it and then turn up the air conditioning. Is it just me, or is it warm in here?

Every radio channel seems to have commercials on, so I plug in my phone and put on some music. I can't settle. I glance at the clock again, and jump when someone knocks on the passenger's side window. I lean over and open the door for Naomi and she slides in.

"Hey," she said.

"You're done early."

She looks at her phone. "Seven whole minutes," she says with her eyebrow raised. "Are you sure you want to fake-marry such a rebel?"

"What can I say, trouble excites me," I grin, turning the

engine on and revving it as I wiggle my eyebrows. Naomi laughs, and I know I'd do anything to make her smile again.

"So where are we going? You look nice," she says, eyeing my shirt and dress pants. "Thanks for the warning," she says as she smooths her skirt over her legs.

"I'm taking you out."

"Is that all I get? No hints, no nothing?"

"No nothing," I grin as I pull out of the parking spot. "Just relax."

"Wow, my fake fiancé is fake wooing me, I like it."

"Will you stop calling me your fake fiancé?" I laugh. "It's weird."

"It's true," she retorts, glancing at me. "I thought we were just discussing the terms of our agreement, I didn't know this was, you know, a *date*."

"Is that a bad thing? We should get to know each other a little if this is going to work. And it should be as realistic as possible."

Naomi doesn't answer, she just shoots me a side-eye look and takes a deep breath. My heart squeezes, and I stare out the windscreen. It feels like all the blood in my body is rushing between my legs and I can't think straight.

"So you're not telling me where we're going?" She asks, peering out the window.

"No, it's a surprise."

"Well, if we're getting to know each other, one thing you should know about me is that I hate surprises."

"Oh yeah?"

"Yeah," she replies, glancing at me. "So last night was basically my worst nightmare. You owe me, big time."

"Big time, eh?" I grin. Her eyes sparkle and her lips tug at the corners.

"Uh-huh," she nods. "I saved your ass. In fact, I'm *still* saving your ass."

"Out of the goodness of your heart?" I ask, turning down a side street towards the restaurant. I'm taking her to New York's hottest new Japanese-fusion degustation restaurant. It's not even open to the public yet, and I can't wait to take Naomi. When she said she'd go out with me tonight, I knew I'd take her here.

"Yes, saving your ass out of the goodness of my heart," she laughs. "I'm just a great person, you know."

"Nothing to do with the two hundred and fifty grand coming your way?"

"Three hundred, after last night," she grins. "That's the fee for surprises."

"Right," I chuckle. "You drive a hard bargain."

She turns towards me and her eyes flash. She lets her gaze drop down my body and a blush creeps over her cheeks, and then she turns away, leaning her arm against the window. She bites her lip and a thrill rushes through my body.

I want her.

Ever since we kissed, I haven't been able to think about anything except her lips, and the feeling of her body against mine.

Naomi takes a deep breath, turning towards me. "Listen, Max, about last night—"

"It's okay," I say. "You don't have to say it."

"No, I do. I just think that if we're going to do this whole engagement thing, we can't be getting involved. It'll just be too complicated. We need to just treat this like a business relationship. You know, with boundaries. Like we can kiss and be affectionate in public when necessary, but that's where we should draw the line. Nothing... you know. Last night..." She takes a deep breath.

"You're right," I say. "I agree," even though I hate the thought of never kissing her again.

I make another turn and stop outside a nondescript black door. A valet appears, and I drop my keys in her hand. Another valet opens Naomi's door and helps her out of the car. She stands up, glancing towards me over the roof of the car with wide eyes.

I adjust my shirt and walk over to her, holding out my arm for her. She hooks her hand into the crook of my elbow, leaning into me.

"Is this Yomoyori?" She whispers as a thick black curtain is opened for us. I put my hand over hers and squeeze it. She looks up at me, jaw agape. "I'm not dressed for this."

"You look incredible, Naomi," I grin. She's wearing a simple black dress, and against her pale skin and red hair it makes her look like a goddess.

But I might be biased, I think she looks incredible in her work uniform, too.

The Maitre D greets us and ushers us through a sensual, dark foyer and towards a booth at the back of the restaurant. Waiters bring wine and menus to start, and explain how the degustation is going to work. When they walk away, Naomi grins and shakes her head. A candle on the table flickers, giving her skin a soft, ethereal glow.

"I can't believe you've taken me here," she says. "I didn't even know this was open yet!"

"It's not," I answer. "Well, not really. I know the chef."

"Of course you do," she laughs as the waiter brings the first course. He rattles off a string of ingredients that I don't listen to, and pours us a new wine to pair with the food.

"Thank you," Naomi smiles at him, and then turns to me, shaking her head. "This is supposed to be a business dinner."

"Is it?"

"Yes," she laughs. "But this food does look delicious, so I'll allow it."

"We can talk business if you want, but I thought it would be nice to, you know, act like a couple. Might make it easier to pretend like we're together if we've done the whole first date awkward questions thing already."

Naomi grins, sipping her wine and shaking her head.

"What kind of first dates have you been on? What's the 'first date awkward questions thing'?"

"You know, you'll ask me about my ex, and I'll answer that we just parted ways or some generic answer that doesn't mean anything, and then you'll tell me about your ex. Then we'll ask each other how many siblings we have. We'll talk about a lot of things that don't really matter, but we'll know a lot of facts about each other."

"We've already covered both of those." Naomi's eyes look dark in the candlelight. "You told me about your ex, and we're both only children."

"Right. Well, I don't know then," I pick up the wine glass, looking at the dark red liquid for answers. "What's your favorite color?"

"Well, I'm not six years old, so I don't have one," Naomi laughs. "Do people actually ask each other these things? Is this what dating is like?"

I laugh along with her, shaking my head. "I don't know, I'm usually half-cut at a bar when I'm talking to women. They usually just want my money, and I usually just want sex. This," I gesture between the two of us. "I'm not sure how to qualify this."

"Stop trying to put me in a box," she says, staring at me over her wine. She glances down at her food and picks up her fork, grinning at me. "We're wasting precious eating time talking about things that don't matter."

"True."

Naomi takes a bite, closing her eyes and moaning as the food hits her tongue. My cock jumps in my pants, and I shift in my seat. She moans again, nodding and pointing her fork at the plate. I take my first bite, and it's my turn to moan. We chew, nodding at each other, pointing at the food, and moving our eyebrows, quickly dissolving into laughter.

I wash down the food with wine, and then I reach my hand across the table. Naomi puts her palm against mine, staring into my eyes.

I take a moment to build up the courage to ask her something real. She's staring at me as if she's expecting it, so I take a deep breath and go for it.

"What made you change your mind?"

16

NAOMI

"What do you mean?" I know what he means, but I'm stalling.

"About this whole thing. About us—about me. When I left you yesterday morning, you looked like you were going to say no. And then after you saw your mom, you told me you'd do it."

I pull my hand away from his, grabbing my wine glass and taking a sip. When I put it back down, the waiter appears with our second course. I try to listen to him explain what the second course in front of me is, but most of it doesn't look like any kind of dinner I've had before.

We thank him, and he leaves.

Max is still staring at me, and the question hangs between us. I'm not sure what to say. I hardly know this guy—should I tell him about my mom? We've agreed to do this crazy engagement, but the whole thing could blow up in my face.

Do I trust Max enough to open up to him?

I take a deep breath, looking at him again. His eyes are soft, and he's waiting patiently for me to speak. A wave of comfort washes over me, and I think about what he said when we first got here. If this whole charade is going to work, we're going to have to act like a couple.

I'm going to have to open up to him.

"I found out my mom has breast cancer," I say, staring at my plate. There's a single asparagus balancing on what looks like a fancy meatball. "She told me when I confronted her about foreclosure notice I found on Sunday."

My voice chokes as the words stick to my throat. I clear my throat, washing down the pain with a sip of wine.

"I'm so sorry," Max says. He looks down at the table between us, staring at nothing. "I'm sorry. If I'd have known, I wouldn't have—I don't want to put you in this position."

"No!" I say, maybe a bit too loud. "This is helping me out. I —" *I want this?* "I need the money."

"Right."

"And plus," I say, stabbing the fancy meatball. "Hanging out with you is alright."

His eyes flick up towards me and a grin appears on his perfect lips. How is it possible for one man to be so handsome? He forks his own meatball and nods to me.

"Hanging out with you isn't so bad, either."

I laugh, blinking back the tears that had misted my eyes when I mentioned my mom. "Good. That means we're miles ahead of half the married couples out there already."

The meatball tastes incredible. I don't know what they've done, but it's so packed with flavor that I can't help but close my eyes and grunt in satisfaction. I've never tasted food this good.

"So last night," I start. "Your parents."

"I'm so, so sorry about that," Max interrupts.

I laugh. "It's okay," I say, shaking my head. "To be honest, it looked like it was as hard for you as it was for me."

Max blows the air out of his mouth, leaning back in his

chair and running his fingers through his thick, black hair. His eyes look almost navy in this light, and the candlelight is making his jaw look like it's chiseled from marble. A delicious tingle of energy passes through my spine and settles in the base of my stomach.

"Why do they want you to get married so badly?"

"I'm not sure," Max says. He looks at me, cocking his head to the side. "They've always been putting pressure on me, but this time..."

"What?" I ask gently when he stops.

"I don't know. I feel like there's something else going on. I can't put my finger on it. I mean, they've always been... overbearing? That's not the right word. They've always been *involved*, I guess. But they've never shown up without warning or told me that I needed to get married or get fucking *disowned*."

He chuckles bitterly, shaking his head.

"I mean, I shouldn't complain. It could be worse." He looks at me, and I smile sadly.

"Yeah."

The next couple of courses are as delicious as the first two, and our conversation turns to lighter things. He tells me about his work, and his knee, and about college football. I tell him about Meg and Ariana, and about how I got into physical therapy.

Conversation is easy. We laugh and joke. He gets my sarcasm, and quips back whenever I say something snarky. It's fun.

By the time dessert comes, he's talking about his injury.

"I was supposed to be in the NFL the year after. We were winning the championship and then I got tackled from behind and my knee just snapped. It wasn't just my knee," he says, staring into his wine glass. "I mean, my whole future was destroyed. NFL, football, my girlfriend left me," he sighs. "It was a hard time."

"I'm so sorry, Max," I say, reaching over to put my hand on his arm. Even though I told him I didn't want to do anything sexual with him, the electricity courses through my body when we touch. He puts his hand over mine, and we stay like that for a few minutes.

This dinner—it's intimate. I'm enjoying it more than I thought I would. We haven't discussed the business arrangements at all; we've just basically been on a date.

I should be worried about that, or worried about what that means, but all I can think about is how much I'm enjoying just being with him. And how much I'm enjoying the heat of his broad palm against my hand.

Max smiles at me, shaking his head. "It's fine. I'm tough."

I grin. "Right."

"I bounce back, you know. Land on my feet."

"Like a cat."

"Exactly."

We laugh, and my heart squeezes. This is so easy.

It's too easy.

Too easy to slip into something else—something beyond a simple transaction. Too easy to make this complicated, and messy.

Too easy to do all the things I'm dying to do, to give in to the temptation that's buzzing through my body anytime he's around.

He pulls his hand away, and I clear my throat, smoothing my hands down the front of my dress.

"Should we go?" He asks, and I nod. I don't trust my voice right now, so I just gather my things and take his outstretched hand, following him back to the car.

17

MAX

EVEN THOUGH WE didn't discuss the intricate details of our arrangement last night, I still get my lawyer to draft up a contract. I send it to Naomi for her to review, with a note saying to change anything that might jump out at her.

Once it's signed, our agreement will be legally binding. She'll be pretending to be my fiancée for one month, with the option to extend for another month. I'll pay her three hundred thousand dollars the first month, and two hundred and fifty the second.

It feels strange to send the contract to her. Last night felt almost like a date, and now I'm sending a cold, emotionless contract. I can't make sense of it in my brain. It's like the two images just don't fit together.

I wanted to kiss her goodbye last night, but we agreed to keep physical contact to a minimum. I lean back in my chair at the office, interlacing my fingers behind my head and thinking of her face when I dropped her off.

"Well, thanks," she'd said, smiling shyly. I'd nodded, and then she'd stuck out her hand. We laughed when we shook hands, and then she turned around and went up the steps to her apartment.

I jump when my assistant opens my office door.

"You have a call on line two," she says, and then chews her lip.

"What is it, Allie?"

"It's your mother."

"Right," I sigh. "Thanks for the heads up."

She nods and slips back out the door. I take a deep breath, checking my computer to make sure the contract has gone through to Naomi, and then I pick up the phone.

"Hello, Mother."

"Max, how many times have I told you not to call me that!"

"Well, you are my mother, aren't you?"

"You're irreverent."

"You say that like it's a bad thing."

I hear her take a deep breath, and I imagine her pinching the bridge of her nose with her perfectly manicured nails. She lets the breath out slowly, and when she speaks, her voice is calm.

"I'd like to take you and Naomi out to dinner. I think it would be good for us all to get to know each other better."

I'm not so sure about that.

"She's pretty busy these days, the clinic is—"

"Just ask her, Max. I have a reservation at Per Se for tomorrow night."

"Right, so you're not really asking me, you're telling me that we're going out to dinner."

She sighs again. "This is important."

"I'm sure it is," I say. "I gotta go, I've got a meeting to get to."

I slam the phone down, pushing my chair back and standing up. I pace back and forth, trying to let the frustration dissipate. This is typical Carol Westbrook! She just bulldozes everyone and everything around her to get what she wants. No doubt we'll end up going to the fancy French restaurant tomorrow night, and she'll grill Naomi on her entire life story.

It'll be uncomfortable and unnecessary. This whole thing is unnecessary! There's no need for me to get married so quickly!

I glance at the phone on my desk again, frowning. Walking back to the other side of my desk, I dial my father's phone number.

He picks up on the third ring. "Hello, son."

"Dad," I say, almost breathless. "I need to talk to you. Are you free?"

"Well, I—"

"It's important."

"I was just going to go up to Konnect to hit a couple golf balls. You can meet me there if you want?"

Typical. The only way my father could get away from my mother long enough to do anything in New York was to play golf.

"I'll meet you there."

MY DAD CAN FIND a golf course anywhere—even in the middle of Manhattan. The indoor golf center is just around the corner from the Rockefeller Center, and it doesn't take long for me to get there.

When I arrive, he's already whacking golf balls and drinking a tumbler of bourbon, surrounded by some of his friends and business associates. I imagine many business deals happen in places like this, under the guise of some leisurely golf practice.

My father's cheeks are rosy, and the tip of his nose is red. That's probably his second or third bourbon. He sees me and spreads his arms, beckoning me forward.

"Max! Max get over here," he booms in the voice he uses when he's surrounded by people who admire him. "Fellas, I want you to meet my son. If he's lucky, he might be where I am now in a couple years."

I stretch a smile over my face and shake hands with the men, trying to remember which one is Jim, or Bill, or Jerry. We exchange pleasantries until I can pull my father away from them. I lead him towards the bar, and we slide onto bar stools before beckoning the bartender over for another round of drinks. My father stares at the amber liquid left in his glass, and then turns to me. He stares at me through one eye and then huffs.

"So?" He asks.

My heart starts thumping, and I hate myself for being nervous to talk to my dad. I take a deep breath, accepting the drink that the bartender places in front of me. I turn to my dad.

"Why are you so desperate for me to get married? I mean, showing up at my house on Sunday? Coming to the city on such short notice? *Staying* in the city? What's going on?"

My father purses his lips, glancing towards the booth where his friends are laughing and patting each other on the shoulders. He turns back towards me and nods his head towards them.

"You see Jerry over there?"

I try to remember which one Jerry was, and I nod.

"We're in the middle of an important acquisition. Jerry's

company is going to become our new international oil and gas materials division. I want you to head it."

My eyebrows shoot up and I snap my jaw closed, trying to erase the shock from my face.

"I... what?"

"You've been doing well. Everyone can see it. Your numbers this quarter are the best we've seen in years. You're ready."

"Two days ago you were threatening to fire me, and now you're telling me you're planning to promote me?"

None of this makes sense. The acquisition, the pressure to get married, none of it.

My father takes a deep breath, as if he's explaining something to someone incredibly dense. He might as well be, because I don't exactly feel bright right now.

"Son, this position will have you traveling all over the world. You'll be meeting diplomats and dignitaries, and business leaders from all over the world. Do you know why there hasn't been a President without a First Lady?"

"Because we live in a nation with backwards ideas about family and success?"

He sighs, rolling his eyes and shaking his head.

"It's comments like that that make me doubt your abilities as a leader of this company, Max. I haven't worked my whole life to watch you tear it all down."

"I'm not tearing anything down, Dad," I respond. "You're a businessman, not a family planner."

"Single men aren't accepted in these circles," he says, frustrated. He looks me square in the eye, taking a deep breath. "You don't have to love her. I mean, lord knows I've had some trying times with your mother. But she does have to be there. She's just as important to the success of this company as you are."

"So this... this is *business*?! All this pressure to get married?"

"You're only realizing that now?" He shakes his head, laughing bitterly. "Welcome to the real world, son."

I say nothing, and my dad takes his drink, nodding to his friends—business partners—whatever they are.

"You want to hit a couple balls before you go back?"

"Nah, Dad, I'm good," I say, finishing my drink. "Lots to do at the office."

"Of course." He pauses, turning back towards me. "Your mother has a dinner planned tomorrow night. You understand that we need to make sure she's a suitable match, don't you?"

Anger burns inside me. A *suitable match*? What is this, the fourteen-hundreds? Am I the fucking King of England or something? Last time I checked, it was the twenty-first century! Since when are wives necessary for high-ranking positions?!

I leave some money on the bar and try to stalk out of the golf center. My dad calls me over, slapping his hand on one of the guy's back. I think it's Jerry.

"Max, come over here!"

"I hear you're celebrating your new engagement, congratulations," Jerry says, eyeing me with a sly grin. "Hope she's a good one."

"Otherwise she'll make your life a living hell, believe me," Jim—or is it Bill?—guffaws. The men laugh, and a tendril of disgust curls in my stomach. I grin, tolerating their pleasantries for a few more minutes before excusing myself.

I'll walk back to the office. The fresh air and noise will help drown out the chaotic thoughts swirling in my head. All this pressure for me to get married, all the phone calls and badgering I've endured—it's all because of a business deal?

I'm not entirely surprised. This company is my parents' entire life. But I'm supposed to just play along with their plan?

I hate myself for agreeing to this. I hate myself for stringing Naomi along with me, and I hate my parents for forcing me into this. But at the end of the day, I know I don't want them to cut me off. I don't want them to shut me out of my entire inheritance and the entire society that I've grown up in.

I need to play along, at least for now.

18

NAOMI

"I've got flashcards," I say when Max opens the door. He looks tired, but his eyes spark and a smile twitches over his lips.

"Flashcards?"

"Yep." I dig around my huge tote, pulling out the stack of cards that's held together with a thick elastic band. I run my thumb over the edge, making the cards slap together.

"What are the flashcards for?" Max closes the door behind me and slides onto a bar stool at the kitchen island. I take the one next to him, fishing out a bottle of wine and dropping my bag on the floor.

"They're for studying. They've got facts about me, and stories about my childhood, and things that people who are engaged might know about each other. I brought blank ones for you to write on, too. And we can come up with a back story."

Max is eyeing me as a smile plays in his eyes. I clear my throat, taking the elastic band off and reading the first card.

"Why did I get suspended from school in third grade?"

His smile widens as his eyebrow arches. He shrugs,

sliding off the stool. "I'm not sure," he says, heading towards the glass cabinet that contains expensive-looking wine glasses. He takes two out, placing them on the marble in front of me.

"Well, I started buying candy in bulk at the grocery store and re-selling it to the kids at recess."

"That's very entrepreneurial of you," he grins as he digs around a drawer. He pulls out a corkscrew, and I laugh. I pick up the bottle, twisting the top open.

"Look at you, with your fancy corkscrew," I grin. "Twist-off." I lift the bottle up and pour some in his glass, before hesitating. "Do you want me to let the tannins mellow, or whatever? Am I supposed to let this breathe?"

"I'm sure it's fine." He picks up the glass and sniffs it, nodding.

"Well, you're the one with the fancy-pants corkscrew," I laugh. "I can't afford wines that don't twist off."

He slides back into the bar stool next to me. The warmth of his body makes my head spin. "So tell me about this candy cartel you had."

"Funny you should say that," I answer, filling up my glass. "I got caught because I hired a couple people to distribute. They started talking a bit too much, and a teacher overheard.

"Is your last name Escobar?"

"Might as well be," I laugh. "I was suspended for three days for that."

"Doesn't look like it impacted your future."

"My mom was so mad," I laugh. "She's like, an artsy-fartsy type of person. She's a painter. She couldn't believe that I would stoop down to dirty, dirty capitalism."

"I don't think your mom would like my parents," he grins. "They are the epitome of capitalism." He takes a sip of wine and his eyebrows raise. "That's not bad, actually." He looks at his glass with appreciation.

"You know, they had this experiment where they had the top sommeliers in the world taste the most expensive wines and the cheapest ones, and a lot of them couldn't tell the difference."

"Oh yeah?"

"Yeah. Don't ask me any details about it though, because I don't know them." I laugh. "So you shouldn't turn your nose up at my humble twist-off bottle."

"I'm not turning my nose up at anything," Max says, leaning against the counter and staring at me. His eyes drop to my lips. A shiver passes down my spine and I clear my throat.

I came here after Max called me and told me his mother had a dinner planned for tomorrow. I was prepared to tell him about my life, to learn about his, and to come up with a believable back story for us. I printed and signed the contract.

I'm here to get paid. I'll pretend to be his fiancée for a month, maybe two, and I'll have enough money to pay for my mom's treatments. It's supposed to be simple.

But it's not.

Right here is where he kissed me. Where *I* kissed *him*. In his house—this is where I felt my whole body turn to liquid heat as his hands sank into my hips and pulled me into him.

Every time he looks at me, I need to squeeze my thighs together to try to ignore the desire that flames to life inside me.

I clear my throat.

"What about you, you ever been suspended?"

"No," he replies. "Model student."

"Of course," I say, rolling my eyes. "Mr. Goodie-Two-Shoes."

"I did light a small campfire on the school grounds, but I ran away when a teacher came to investigate. My friend Joel took the blame."

I drop my jaw in mock horror. "You let your friend take the fall for you?"

"I know, I know. Coward."

"Awful. I might have to call this wedding off."

He grins, leaning closer to me. His eyes are glued on mine and I can't look away. I don't want to look away. I want to get lost in the blue depths of his gaze and melt against him. I want to smell his hair and feel my skin spark when he touches me.

As if he can read my mind, he puts his hand on my thigh. Even through my jeans, the heat of the contact makes my head spin. The space between my legs turns to fire as my heartbeat races in my chest.

It would be so easy to kiss him—and more. I could just lean over and press my lips against his. I could let my body do the talking, and run my fingers over his chiseled chest. I could reach down between his legs and feel his length against my palm, and do all the things that my body is begging me to do.

Instead, I glance down and take a sip of wine. I grab my bag from the floor and fish out the thick contract. Max straightens, clearing his throat and taking a sip of wine. He drops his hand from my thigh and I miss his touch the instant his hand slips away.

"I signed this."

"Did you have a lawyer look it over?"

I laugh. "Yes, I called the lawyer I have on retainer. She cleared her schedule to look it over." I glance at him, eyebrow raised. "You and I live in very different worlds, Mr. Westbrook." He grins, and I continue. "I read it, and it seems fine. It's signed, anyways. Here."

I slide the papers over, and he pushes them to the side. "I'm more interested in the flashcards right now."

My heart flutters and my lips twitch into a grin. I nod, handing him a stack of blank ones. "Write down some facts about yourself. We need to come up with a good story about how we met."

"We met at physio."

"I know, but we need *details*. How, when, what's happened since then. That kind of thing. I only met your mom for a few minutes, but she won't be satisfied with 'we met at physio'."

Max chuckles and nods. "That's probably true."

"Did you ask them why they want you to get married so badly? You told me you thought it was weird, even for them."

He looks away from me, shifting uncomfortably in his seat. "No, not yet." I wait for him to continue, but he doesn't.

Not wanting to push the issue, I just nod.

"Okay, come on, let's get to work." I fish out a pen from my bag and hand it to him. I top off our wine and try to forget about the ache between my legs and the fire in my veins.

19

MAX

My heart skips a beat when Naomi appears at her apartment door. She looks incredible. Her red hair is falling in loose waves around her shoulders, and the way her navy dress is hugging every curve is doing crazy things to my body. Earrings are glittering next to her face as she tucks her hair behind her ear, clutching a small purse an making her way down the steps.

I jump to stretch my arm out to her, leaning down to kiss her cheek.

God, she smells incredible.

"Hey," she says, smiling.

"Hey."

I open the door for her, watching her move fluidly as she sits down in the passenger's seat. She smiles at me as I close the door and jog to the driver's side.

"You look beautiful," I say when I get in.

"Is this okay for meeting the parents?"

"It's okay for anything," I answer. She could wear a paper bag and she'd look perfect. We drive in silence for a while, and then Naomi takes a deep breath. When she says nothing, I clear my throat.

"What's up?" I ask, reaching over to touch her leg. She puts her hand over mine, forcing a smile on her lips as she glances at me.

"I'm nervous. I've never been a great actor. Or liar."

"Just be yourself. We'll keep the lying to a minimum, and I'll do my best to keep the conversation neutral. Okay?"

"Okay."

I squeeze my hand over her leg, and she takes another deep breath. By the time we make it to the restaurant, she's still tense. She's holding my hand though, and I'm not complaining about that. I drop the keys with the valet and lead her inside. We're ushered to my parents, who are waiting with a bottle of champagne already uncorked and ready for us.

My mother stands up and stretches her arms out in the type of exaggerated affection that she reserves for public appearances. She kisses both my cheeks and I turn to shake my dad's hand. My mom turns to Naomi, who stumbles through the kissing charade and giggles nervously, leaning over to kiss my dad's cheek.

Once we're settled, I reach under the white tablecloth to squeeze Naomi's hand. The waiter pours us some champagne and my mother raises her glass.

"A toast," she proclaims. "To your happiness."

"To your happiness," my father grunts.

"And yours," Naomi replies graciously. We all clink our delicate crystal flutes and take a sip. Frustration burns in the pit of my stomach as the fakeness of the whole interaction starts to bother me. I can't even imagine how Naomi must feel.

None of this is real—not the engagement, not my parents

pretending to take an interest in our happiness, not the forced affection in their relationship. And yet, it still sends warmth coursing through my veins when Naomi squeezes my hand under the table. My eyes soften when I look at her, and my heart jumps when she flicks her beautiful green eyes in my direction.

I want to kiss her.

I want to do a lot more than kiss her, but right now, I'd settle for a kiss. She's wearing soft pink lipstick, and her lips look so incredibly kissable it's making it hard to think about anything else.

"So, tell me about yourself, Naomi," my mother says. Her voice is neutral and she has a smile on her lips, but I know this is the start of the test. She approves of the way Naomi looks, that much is clear, but now the real minefield begins.

Naomi smiles, folding her hands in her lap. "Well," she starts, "I grew up about two hours from the city, with my mom. We grew up in the country growing our own vegetables. My mom's a painter—I guess you could call her a hippie. I couldn't have had a more different upbringing than Max," she laughs. "But maybe that's why we get along so well." She puts her hand on my forearm. "Don't they say opposites attract?"

"They do say that," my dad grunts.

"And now you're a physical therapist?"

"I am. I went to college in Ithaca and moved to the city about oh—almost eight years ago. Our physical therapy practice is one of the best in the city. We get lots of professional athletes and high-level clients coming through. I've been lucky."

"You've worked hard, I'm sure."

"Of course." Naomi smiles, taking a sip of champagne. I squeeze her hand under the table again, clearing my throat.

"So, Mom, how's that fundraiser going? Which charity are you working on now?"

My mother smiles, turning to Naomi. She talks about her charitable donations for the next fifteen minutes with minimal prodding and encouragement from the rest of us.

When all else fails, get her to talk about herself. I learned that a long time ago.

Finally, the meal draws to an end. We order coffees after dinner, and Naomi leans back in her chair. She sighs, and I can see the tiredness lining her face.

Maybe it's having a dinner like this after a full day of work, or maybe it's just the effort of pretending to be engaged when she isn't. I put my arm around her chair, kissing her temple.

God, she smells good.

She leans into me. "We'll go soon," I whisper in her ear. She nods slightly, and smiles at me.

My father clears his throat, reaching into his jacket's breast pocket. He pulls out a little black velvet box, putting it down in the center of the table.

"That's for you, Naomi," he grunts. My eyes widen and I look from him to my mother. She nods, her lips pressed into a thin, self-satisfied smile.

"Go ahead," she says.

Naomi looks at me with wide eyes, and then reaches hesitantly towards the box. She opens it up as a lump forms in my throat.

I don't need to look—I already know what it is. Still, when she opens it and I see the bright green emerald surrounded with dozens of brilliant diamonds. The gems sparkle in the restaurant's low light, and my heart skips a beat.

"Oh my goodness," Naomi breathes. Her eyes are shining and they're as wide as dinner plates. She shakes her head, snapping the box closed. "I can't accept this," she says, pushing the box back towards my dad. He clears his throat, drawing his thick eyebrows closer together. My mother straightens in her chair, her mouth opening slightly.

"What do you mean, Naomi?"

"I just..." Naomi looks at me and I see the panic in her eyes. "It's too much. I can't..."

"Of course you can," my mother says, pushing the box back towards her.

"That was my mother's ring," Dad explains. "It's been in the family for almost a hundred years. I noticed you aren't wearing an engagement ring yet, I thought Max would have explained." He looks at me, nodding his chin down slightly.

I take the little box in my hand, feeling the smooth velvet under my fingertips as I flick it open. I take the delicate ring from it, remembering how my grandmother used to cherish it.

Turning to Naomi, I meet her gaze. Her eyes are still as wide as I've ever seen them, as if she's trying to keep the panic from spilling out of her. I take her left hand in mine, giving it a gentle squeeze. She's trembling, and my chest squeezes.

I glance at my parents, who are staring at us expectantly. Tears are forming in Naomi's eyes as I bring the ring towards her left hand.

It slides onto her finger as if it was made for her. My mother grunts appreciatively and my dad crosses his arms over his chest. I see him nod in my peripheral vision.

My eyes are glued on Naomi's. Her mouth has dropped open. She glances at the ring on her finger, her eyes widening ever so slightly.

I put a finger on her chin, tilting it up towards me. I lay a soft kiss on her lips, running my fingers along her jaw and pulling away after only a second. She clears her throat, glancing at the ring, and then at me, and then at my parents.

"Thank you," she finally says. "I wasn't expecting this."

"Welcome to the family," my mother says with a benevolent smile.

20

NAOMI

I TAKE the ring off as soon as I get home, placing it back in its little black box and shoving the box in my underwear drawer. I curl up on my bed, eyeing my dresser suspiciously.

This is too much.

I knew this was a bad idea. *'Welcome to the family'*?! It sounds like something an Italian mafioso would say. What have I gotten myself into? What will happen when we have to 'break it off'? What will Max say to them? What will *they* say to *me*?! I didn't know how connected—how rich—they were before all this. I had an idea, but I didn't *know*. Would they be vindictive? Would they go after me?

We should have worked all these things out beforehand. Now it's too late. We can't go back. I'm part of the family now, for fuck's sake!

I jump up, heading to my kitchen. I stand in the middle of the room with one hand on my hip and the other on my forehead. I stare at a spot on the wall, thinking of nothing and everything all at once.

My phone rings, and I practically jump out of my skin. My heart races until I see Meg's number on the screen.

"Hey," I answer.

"How'd it go?"

"Oh my god," I answer, sinking into a chair. "Meg, they gave me a family heirloom."

"What?!"

"Yeah. His grandmother's ring."

Meg laughs. "So it went well, then."

"This is such a bad idea."

"Well, yeah, obviously," she laughs. "I could have told you that days ago. In fact, I think I *did* tell you that days ago. Maybe the first time I saw that little flirtation between the two of you."

"There's no flirtation," I say.

"Yeah, right. And Ariana is a celibate monk."

I laugh. "Fine. But we *agreed*. Business is business. No sex. No kissing in private."

"Uh-huh."

"It's true!"

"Uh-huh."

"I'm not doing anything with him."

"Uh-huh."

"Meg."

"Naomi."

I huff, and try to stop the smile spreading across my face. "I'll tell you everything at work tomorrow."

"Bring the ring, I want to see it."

"I'm not bringing that ring anywhere. Can you imagine if I lost it? I'm terrified of wearing it anywhere."

"Send me a picture, then."

"Okay," I grin. "See you in the morning."

I hang up and bite my lip. Clutching my phone to my chest, I tip-toe back towards my bedroom. I look at the dresser, breathing deeply. Shaking my head, I gather the courage to open my underwear drawer. I fish out the little black velvet box and put it on top of the dresser. I flick on a light and take a picture of it, sending it to Meg and Ariana.

It only takes a few seconds for them to answer with exclamations about size and carats and cost. I shut the box up again and stuff it back with my undies, curling up in bed and answering the texts. My eyelids are heavy and the panic in my chest has subsided with my friends' help when my phone buzzes again. It's Max.

Goodnight, beautiful. Thank you for tonight.

I'd be lying if I said my heart didn't skip a beat. I smile despite myself and answer him right away, putting my phone on the nightstand and closing my eyes. I see his face painted on my eyelids, and the way he looked in that crisp white shirt of his. I see the cut of his jaw and the way his biceps bulged against the fabric of his top.

Sighing, I try to ignore the tendril of desire that curls in my stomach every time I think of him.

I WAKE up to banging on my door.

"Naomi! Naomi, open up!"

I frown, rolling over in bed and squinting at my alarm clock. Six in the morning.

"Naomi! I know you're in there!"

"Mom?" I mumble. Is that my mother's voice? What is she doing in the city? What is she doing at *my house*?! The banging on the door continues until I stumble out of bed and wrap a housecoat around myself.

"Coming!" I yell, and the banging subsides. I rub the sleep from my eyes and stifle a yawn as I make my way to the door.

I shuffle along the rug, listening hard for noise on the other side of the door.

I open my door and my mother rushes past me in a flurry of anger and outrage.

"Finally! I've been knocking on your door for ages!"

"I was asleep."

"What is this about?!" She says, brandishing a newspaper in front of me. Her hands are shaking and I can't make out the headline.

"What's what about?"

"This!" She says, waving the newspaper harder. "You're *engaged*?! To Max *Westbrook*?!"

My heart drops to my stomach. My throat tightens and my palms get sweaty.

I need coffee. I can't handle this right now.

I take a deep breath, looking at my mother's disheveled hair and the anger flashing in her eyes. She looks down at the newspaper, handing it to me. I take it from her and see the headline:

Heir to Billion-Dollar Fortune Engaged to Physical Therapist

My heart hammers in my chest, and I avoid my mother's eye. There's a photo of me and Max leaving the restaurant last night. His parents are behind us. I remember the flashing of cameras and Max's hand on the small of my back as he ushered me into his car, but I didn't think that this would happen. I didn't think I'd be in the news! Is this news nowadays?

"Did you drive all the way here to ask me about some newspaper article?"

"No," she replies, taking a deep breath. "I have a doctor's appointment this morning."

"You never told me that. Your doctor's in the city?"

"Stop stalling," She stabs the newspaper. "What's going on?"

My mother stares at me expectantly, so I take a deep breath and turn towards the kitchen.

"You want coffee?"

"No, I do not want coffee," she proclaims. "I want you to explain what the heck is going on here! You never wanted to get married!"

"No, Mom," I say as I spin on my heels towards her. "*You* never wanted me to get married because *you* don't believe in marriage. You never actually asked me what I want!"

She looks taken aback. Her hand flies to her chest as her eyebrows jump up. Her mouth opens and then closes again, and I immediately regret my outburst.

"I'm sorry, I didn't mean—"

"No, you're right," she says, a little bit more softly. "I'm just... I'm just surprised is all. I didn't even know you had a boyfriend."

She frowns and I turn back towards the kitchen to make some coffee. When the machine starts gurgling, I take a deep breath and face her again. She looks concerned. Her eyebrows are drawn together and her lips are pinched so tight that they're just a thin white line across her face.

"Is this what you want?" She asks. I can hear the pain in her voice.

I hesitate. I could tell her the truth, but where would that get me? She'd never take the money if she knew what I was doing for it, and then this whole thing would be for nothing. And plus, the more people know the truth, the more likely it is that someone will find out, and then, once again, the whole thing would be for nothing.

So I don't tell her the truth. Instead, I try to smile.

"Yeah, it is what I want."

It should feel wrong, saying that. It should feel like I'm lying to my mother and lying to myself. But maybe the most surprising thing of the past week is that it *doesn't* feel wrong. When I say that I want this, it feels like I'm telling the truth.

And that scares me more than anything.

21

MAX

NAOMI'S FACE is plastered all over the newspaper. She looks gorgeous, obviously, but that's not the point. She shouldn't be on the newspaper in the first place. None of us should! Why do people care about my engagement anyway? This stinks of a set-up. The photos look almost staged. How would reporters have known we were at the restaurant last night?

"Did you orchestrate that article?" I ask, reading the headline over and over.

I hear my mother sigh through the phone.

"Max," she starts.

"Did you?"

"You know how the press are."

"You're not answering the question."

"What do you want me to say?"

"I want you to tell me if you set this up!" My voice is getting louder, and I pace back and forth in my living room. "Naomi and I were blindsided!"

"I don't see what the big deal is," she huffs. "You'd have to announce it sometime."

"Yes, Mom," I say, pinching the bridge of my nose. "*We*

would have to announce it. On our terms. Not have it spilled all over the tabloids like this."

"It's hardly a tabloid."

"Mom—"

"Well, it's done now. Everyone knows. I'm already fielding phone calls from *everyone*. I've got a PI looking into her background. To be honest, that would have been better to get done before the article came out, but that's okay."

"You've got *what?!*"

Fuck.

"Well, Max, you didn't think we'd let you marry just anyone without looking into her, would you?"

"I do *not* want you to investigate my fiancée!"

"Max, be reasonable."

I feel like a cartoon character with steam blowing out of my ears. My face feels red and hot. This is infuriating. I take a deep, shaky breath and try to keep my voice steady.

"Mom, *stop*. I do *not* want you to put a private investigator on my fiancée! This isn't about you! This is my life!"

"Oh, grow up, Max," my mom says, finally losing the mask of benevolence that she wears so well. "Of course this is about us. Who do you think will inherit the company? Who do you think will be representing us from now on? And I know you spoke to your father about your new position! So how could we not investigate her! We're just looking for skeletons in the closet, Max. If she has nothing to hide, she has nothing to worry about."

She's not the one with something to hide. What if they find the contract? What if they find out about the engagement?

"It's wrong, Mom."

"Well, it's too late. The PI is already on it."

"Call him off!"

"No."

The word feels like a door slamming in my face. I sink down in a chair, dropping my head in my hand. I hang up the phone and take a deep breath.

What am I going to do? If I fight this too much, she'll know something is up. I can't come clean now, because then they would *definitely* cut me off and fire me, not to mention how they would treat Naomi. All I can do is hope for the best and tell Naomi that we need to be extra careful.

I just need a couple of weeks. Once this acquisition goes through, we can split amicably and I'll already have the new job. Naomi will get her money and hopefully her mother will recover. My parents will leave her alone, and they'll have no choice but to keep me as the head of the new division.

All I need is *time*.

But with a PI snooping around Naomi, how much time do I really have?

What is he going to find?

I brush the thought off as soon as it enters my head. Of course he won't find anything—Naomi is as straight-laced as they get. Maybe something will turn up about her mother— Naomi said she was a hippie, after all, and that would be exactly the kind of thing my parents would be looking for.

But it doesn't matter.

I'm not marrying her mother, I'm marrying *her*.

I tap my phone until Naomi's name comes up, and my hand hovers over the keys. Should I tell her about the private investigator?

My heart starts thumping and my eyebrows draw together. I should tell her. I should be open with her. But what if that spooks her? What if she backs out now that she knows how serious my parents are?

The PI won't find anything, so it's not a problem. He'll

hand my parents a generic report about her college life, her criminal record or lack thereof, and then the report will go in the bottom of a drawer, never to be looked at again.

Telling Naomi about the PI would only worry her more. She's got enough on her plate between my parents, her mom, and pretending to be engaged to me. When she called me about the news article, she seemed upset. She doesn't need anything else to worry about. It'll only upset her more.

My parents are overbearing and intrusive, but knowing just how intrusive they are might be too much for her to handle.

I click my phone's screen off and slide it back in my pocket.

Once the decision is made, it's easy to rationalize it to myself. I stand up, grabbing my keys and heading out the door. I dial Naomi's number on the way out.

"My mom set up the photo shoot outside the restaurant," I tell her, closing my apartment door.

"What?!"

"I know," I say as my chest squeezes. "I'm sorry."

"You really need to stop apologizing for things your parents do."

"Sor—I mean, you're right."

Naomi chuckles, and then sighs. I imagine her biting her lip and staring off out the window. Maybe she's scratching the back of her head like she does when she's deep in thought.

"Oh well, it's done now. My mom knows about the engagement."

My jaw drops slightly as I press the elevator button. "Oh. How... is she okay with it? Does she *know*, or she just knows?"

"She doesn't *know*. If you know what I mean." Naomi laughs. "She thinks it's real. She's getting her head around it."

"What did you tell her."

"I told her that I wanted to marry you."

And do you?

The question jumps to the tip of my tongue just as the elevator dings open. "I'm about to get in an elevator, I'll call you later."

"Alright. We got any other public appearances coming up?" I can hear the grin in her voice.

"Not that I know of," I chuckle. "I'll try to get a heads up if that ever happens again."

"Thanks."

The elevator beeps as I hold the door open, and I let the words tumble out of my mouth. "You wanna hang out sometime? I mean like, dinner? Friday?"

"Your parents want to grill me some more?"

The elevator is beeping constantly now, with the doors banging on my arm as they try to close. "No, just me and you. As an apology for yesterday."

Naomi sighs. There's a pause, and then she chuckles. "What the hell, sure. Friday it is."

"I'll pick you up at your place."

I finally drop my arm and let the doors close. I can't keep the smile off my face. I'm going on a date with my fiancée.

22

NAOMI

THE QUESTIONS ARE INCESSANT. At work, Julia is wide-eyed. When, how, where did my engagement happen? I cringe, hating the lies that I have to tell.

I definitely didn't think this through.

Somehow, I thought that this engagement thing would just be an easy pay check for me. I thought I'd agree to it, meet his parents, and get paid.

That hasn't exactly happened. I've gotten paid—at least that's gone to plan. Max is prompt. The transfer came through the day after the news story about our engagement. But other than that, it's been anything but easy.

We've been 'engaged' for less than a week and there's already been two news articles about us, two evenings with his parents, and now my mother and my boss are asking all kinds of questions.

At least Meg and Ariana know the truth. I don't think I'd be able to manage lying to them.

"You didn't notice anything between them?" Meg says when Julia stares at me. "They've been flirting for weeks!"

"Right, okay," Julia says. "But flirting isn't exactly the same things as getting engaged!"

"It's happened pretty quickly. I didn't think it would be so public."

"Naomi, this is highly unprofessional!"

"I'm sorry."

Julia stares at me, and then glances at Meg. She shakes her head. "I just don't... when... how...". She frowns, and my heart thumps.

Is she going to fire me?

Finally, she just looks at her own engagement ring and takes a deep breath. "I'd better be invited to your wedding."

Meg winks at me and puts her arm around Julia. "Of course you'll be invited to her wedding. Think of all the hot, single, rich bachelors that will be there!"

"I'll be married by then, Meg," Julia says, wiggling the fingers of her left hand at in front of her face. "You literally just went to my bachelorette party."

"I know," Meg laughs, leading her away from me. "But a girl can look, can't she?"

She glances over her shoulder and I mouth the words 'thank you'. Looks like I won't get fired after all. It's a good thing Julia is in the middle of her own wedding craze, otherwise she might be less forgiving.

Clients ask me about it, and my mother calls me again in the evening to make sure I'm okay. The stress is building inside me, and I find myself looking forward to Friday.

To my next fake date with my fake fiancé, although it doesn't feel as fake as I thought it would. The more I tell people that we're engaged, and that I'm happy, the more it feels real.

"Do you love him?" My mother asks over the phone. I'm

glad she's not standing in front of me, because my eyes widen and my jaw drops. My mouth goes dry.

I clear my throat.

"Obviously, Mom, come on." I bluff. "I gotta go anyways. When is your next doctor's appointment? I want to come with you."

She takes the bait, changing the subject and I breathe a bit easier. When I get off the phone to her, I call her bank and arrange a payment for her mortgage. I'll pay off the missed payments and the next six months-worth of mortgage payments, and then I'll give her enough for the first six months of her treatments. That should take the pressure off, and she can focus on getting better.

By the time I've transferred the money to the bank and transferred money for my mother's treatment, more than half of the engagement money is gone. I take a deep breath, hanging up the phone and dropping my head in my hands.

The reality of our situation comes rushing back to me.

It might be difficult. It might be public, and it might be uncomfortable, but it's *necessary*. There's no way I could afford almost two hundred thousand dollars out of pocket, just for my mom's mortgage and the first six months of her treatments. Who knows how much ongoing treatment will cost after she goes through the original chemotherapy and radiation? If she needs to have an operation, how much does that cost? And if anything goes wrong?

My mind starts doing circles around me. I take a deep breath, closing my eyes and letting the tears gather behind my eyelids.

I shouldn't panic. We have money now—we have a buffer. She's out of trouble for the moment, and she can focus on getting better.

I jump when my phone rings. "Mom," I say. "What's going

on, is everything okay?" We'd just hung up less than an hour ago.

"Did you pay off my mortgage and deposit money into my account? I just got the notification from my bank."

"I told you I would help you, Mom."

"Take it back."

"What?!"

"I will not have you putting yourself into debt for me. Take it back and return it to whoever you borrowed it from."

"I didn't borrow it, Mom."

"So where did you get it?!"

"I've... I've been saving," I lie. I cringe.

"You've saved almost two hundred thousand dollars?!"

"I..."

"You should be buying a house or something! Not wasting it on me!"

"It's not wasting it, Mom."

"Does this have anything to do with that engagement of yours? Is he *buying* you?!"

That one hurt, because that exact thought has crossed my mind. My mother is way too smart.

"No! Mom! Please, just focus on getting better. I've been working as a physio for almost a decade! Is it that impossible that I would be saving? What does it matter how I got the money?"

"It matters because that kind of money doesn't just fall from the sky, Naomi. I will not let you put yourself in trouble for me. I'll manage, one way or another. Mrs. Yates just told me she'd let me pick up hours at the hotel to clean, and..."

"What, after your chemo appointments? You'll just go straight from the hospital to the hotel? Come on, Mom." I hear a deep, raking breath, and I soften my voice. "Let me help you."

"You remind me so much of your father sometimes."

My heart starts thumping. She never talks about my dad.

"What? Why? I thought he left you before I was born."

"He did, honey. But he's the type of man that would do things on impulse without thinking of the consequences. Good and bad things. It's part of the reason he was so attractive, and part of the reason he was so successful. It's also why he left us."

My throat tightens. This is the most I've heard her talk about him, ever. I don't even know his *name*.

"Who is he, Mom?"

A sob sounds over the phone and my chest squeezes. My heart is thumping, and I feel like I need to know. I've had this hole in my past for so long, this question mark that never went away, and now, with one simple name, my mom could change it all.

"Mom?"

"Just forget about it, Naomi. He's no good."

"Why don't you let me decide that? Don't you think I deserve to know?"

"It's better this way. Why would you want to know the man who left us?"

My heart shatters all over again. It's the same pain as when I was a little girl who didn't understand why I didn't have a daddy. It's the same pain of watching my friends hug their fathers and knowing I'd never feel that. It's the same pain I saw in my mother's eyes every time I asked.

And that pain silences me now. With everything going on, it just doesn't seem like the right time. I'm not sure I can handle another shock. But is there ever a right time for this kind of thing?

I sigh.

"Okay, Mom. I love you."

"Love you too, honey."

I hang up the phone and clutch it to my chest, closing my eyes and breathing deeply. Questions swirl around my mind about my past, my mother, my father, about Max, and the cancer. I wonder if anything I'm doing is right, or if it'll all blow up in my face.

Then, my phone buzzes with a picture from Max. I open it up, and see the top of a wine bottle. Max is holding the corkscrew above it, grinning at me.

Feeling fancy.

Tears cloud my vision and I cry for a few moments, staring at his goofy face as emotions jostle inside my heart. I shouldn't like him as much as I do, but I can't help it. Before I can answer, another message comes through.

Wish you were here to enjoy it with me.

My heart melts, and I type out an answer before I have time to think of the consequences.

Me too xx

I press send and my heart does cartwheels. I shouldn't be getting closer to him. I know that, but right now, it's the only thing that feels good.

23

MAX

WHEN NAOMI ANSWERS THE DOOR, I push a bouquet of flowers towards her.

"These are for you," I say. A smile lights up her face and she takes the bundle of flowers, shoving her nose into it and inhaling.

"They're gorgeous, Max," she smiles. "Thank you. No one's ever gotten me flowers for a date before." She nods towards the door. "Want to come up while I put these in some water?"

"Sure."

My heart hammers while we go back up the creaky stairs to her apartment. The wallpaper is peeling along the stairway, and there's a faint smell of mildew, but apart from that the building looks clean. Naomi unlocks two deadbolts and opens the door to a tiny one-bedroom apartment.

The furniture is cramped, and there's not much room to move between the living room and the tiny kitchen, but I can see Naomi's touch everywhere. There are pictures of her and her mother, her friends, posters of anatomy and textbooks about physical therapy. There's a yoga mat laid out next to the couch, and a screen with a laptop hooked up to it.

"Is that your TV?"

Naomi glances out from the kitchen, where she's fetching a vase.

"Do people still have TVs these days? I just stream shows online, so I just needed a screen."

"I still have a TV."

"You also have a bread making machine."

"What's wrong with a bread making machine!"

"Have you ever made bread?"

"Fair point," I concede.

Naomi laughs. She comes out with the flowers arranged in a small vase. She puts them down on the coffee table and steps back, smiling.

"They're gorgeous."

"Just like you," I say before I can stop myself. She's wearing a tight green top that makes her skin looks like it's made of porcelain. Her eyes shine as she glances at me, and a blush warms her freckled cheeks. She looks back at the flowers, tucking a strand of wavy red hair behind her ear. Sliding her hands over her short black skirt, she nods to the door.

"Should we go?"

"Sure."

Not that I want to. I'd rather pull her close to me and feel her arms hook around my neck. I'd unzip those tall, black boots of hers and peel the black tights off her perfect legs. I'd worship her body and kiss every inch of it.

Instead, we step back into the chilly New York streets. Autumn is well and truly here, and I can feel the winter chill in the air. I open the car door for her and she smiles as she gets in. We ride to the restaurant in silence, and Naomi reaches over to put her hand on my thigh.

My heart jumps in my chest, and I curl my fingers around hers.

We're both quiet, but it's nice. It's companionable. Neither of us talk about things that don't matter or fill the silence with useless chatter. We're just comfortable with each other.

It's been a long time since I've felt that way.

Or rather—it's been a long time since I've *let* myself feel this way. Ever since Farrah left me after my injury, I haven't really let myself be comfortable with a woman. Even when I almost got married to Heather, it didn't feel real. It didn't feel like this. I was just going through the motions.

As if she can read my mind, Naomi squeezes my thigh and smiles at me.

"What are you thinking about?"

"Just... that this is nice."

Her smile widens and she dips her chin down slightly. "Yeah," she says. "It is."

Conversation is easy when we sit down for dinner. She tells me about growing up in the country, and about going to college. I tell her about boarding school, and about football. We drink too much wine and eat too much food.

"You're going to make me fat," she says as she finishes her plate. "All these dinners out are not good for my waistline."

"Well you've cleared me for jogging, so we can start going for runs together in the morning," I laugh.

"Oh, can we?" She grins. "Bit presumptuous, isn't it? Why would we be doing anything together in the morning?"

I just laugh and pay the bill. She slips her hand into mine and we turn down the street towards Central Park. The night is clear, and we can see a couple stars through the light pollution of the city.

Naomi sighs. "At my mom's place, there are thousands of stars. It's not like this."

"Do you miss it?"

"Living out there? Yes and no. The city has a lot more opportunity, but I always think I'd rather end up in a small town in the country."

She leans into me, her body fitting perfectly beside mine. My heart feels light as we walk, and I can't keep the smile from my face. Naomi glances around and then grins at me.

"Is this another photo op that I don't know about? Should I be worried about photographers hiding in the bushes?"

I laugh, shaking my head. "Only when my mother is around."

"That must have been tough, growing up," she says, almost to herself. "Being in the public eye."

"It wasn't that bad. I was at boarding school with other kids like me for most of my youth. And then when I got older, people started paying attention to me because of football, not because of my parents."

"Still, you didn't exactly have a quiet, normal childhood."

"What, one where my mother has nude models walking around the living room every Thursday night?"

She laughs, pushing her shoulder into mine. "She's an artist! She and her artist friends had sittings on Thursdays. It wasn't sexual or weird or anything."

"Just organic, crunchy, granola-eating dicks in full view."

"Granola-eating dicks?" She laughs. "I can assure you there were no dicks eating anything."

I laugh, glancing at her as we walk. I stop, putting my hand on her hip as she tilts her chin up towards me. The tip of her nose is bright red, and the cold is making her cheeks a rosy pink color. She smiles and her eyes twinkle. Her hands circle around the back of my neck and she tilts her head to the side.

"So are you just going to stand there talking about organic dicks, or are you going to kiss me?"

Warmth blooms in my chest. She doesn't have to ask me twice. I lean down, taking her soft, pink lips between mine. I press my hand on the small of her back and feel her melt into me as she kisses me. Her arms pull me in for a deeper kiss as too many layers of clothing separate us.

I run my fingers along her jaw and tangle them into the hair at the base of her neck. She moans into my mouth and leans into me, kissing me fervently as her fingers sink into my shoulders.

When we fall away from each other, her cheeks are bright pink and her lips are glistening. Her hair is like a wild red mane around her head, and her eyes are sparkling brighter than ever before.

"Come home with me," I growl, my eyes low as I pull her closer to me.

"Okay," she says, laying a soft kiss on my lips. "Let's go home."

24

NAOMI

By the time we get to Max's apartment, my heartbeat has mostly gone back down to normal. We shuffle out of our coats and shoes, and he takes out two long-stemmed wine glasses. Producing a nice bottle of red wine, he grins at me as he uncorks it.

"We'll have to be fancy tonight," he grins. "I don't have any twist-offs for you."

"I'll allow it."

The wine glugs as it pours out of the bottle, and he slides a glass towards me. We clink our glasses together, watching each other over the rim.

He's too far away. He's all the way over there, on the other side of the kitchen island. I slide off my seat and walk over to him, leaving my wine on the countertop. I trail my fingers over his waistband, looking up at him and biting my lip.

I can feel the heat of his skin against my fingertips. His powerful lower abdominal muscles ripple as he moves towards me. His hand circles my waist as his other hand tucks a strand of my unruly hair behind my ear. He rests his forehead against mine, closing his eyes and breathing deeply.

Finally, we kiss. Fireworks explode in my chest as our lips touch. It's like the rain starting when a thunderstorm breaks —sweet relief floods through me while the air is still charged with electricity. His hands leave trails of sparks as they trail down my sides, sinking into my hips and pulling me closer.

A growl rumbles through his chest and sends a shiver through my body. I lean into him, the noise making my body respond instinctively. His lips brush against mine as my fingers crawl up his chest, exploring every ridge of his muscled body.

We move slowly, deliberately. He squeezes my waist with his hand as he cups my cheek, and then lifts me up onto the counter in one smooth motion. I rest my arms on his shoulders, kissing him deeply as he moans. I wrap my legs around his waist, pressing my center towards him.

I know he can feel the heat between my legs—how could he not? I claw at his shirt, pulling it off over his head so I can finally, *finally* see his body. He looks like he's been carved from stone. His skin is stretched over the smooth curves of his shredded body. My fingers trace his muscles, falling down the muscular 'V' that leads me straight to his belt buckle.

He groans as I fumble with it, pushing his hips towards me.

"We don't have to do this," he says, resting his hands on my hips as his eyes search mine. "Before, you said..."

"I know what I said," I interrupt. "I was an idiot. I want this." My fingers unlatch the buckle and slide his belt loose. "I want *you*."

He growls again, closing his eyes as I loosen his belt. When I reach down for his fly and shimmy his pants down, he kicks them away and opens his eyes to watch me.

"Your turn."

His hands are warm and strong as he pulls my shirt off

over my head. As soon as it's off, his arms are wrapped around me and his lips are on my lips, my jaw, my neck. His kisses tumble down to my collarbone as he slides my bra strap off my shoulder.

His thumb traces the line of my bra, sinking in the soft flesh of my breast as my chest heaves with every breath. When he unhooks the clasp of my bra and slides it off my shoulders, his mouth opens slightly and he groans. His thumbs brush my nipples and I shiver.

Every touch is electric. Every sound is heady and intoxicating. Every kiss sends me closer and closer to the edge.

Yes, I want this. I want this more than I've ever wanted anything else.

In this crazy week, with everything that's happening, with all the uncertainty and the lying and pretending, this is the first things that's felt *real*. It's ironic, but it's true.

He wraps his arms around me, lifting me up off the counter and carrying me towards his bedroom. I can feel his length through his boxers, pressed up against my hip crease. I wish I wasn't wearing all this clothing.

Max lays me down on the softest bed I've ever felt, leaning his body over me. He crushes his lips against mine, groaning into our kiss. I pull him closer, arching my back and rolling my hips to feel his hardness against me.

I'm drenched. I'm dripping for him, and all I want is to feel him—*all* of him.

He fumbles with my skirt and tights, kissing me as his fingers work the zipper open. He trails his kisses down my chest, pausing to take each breast in his mouth before moving his kisses down over my stomach. He pulls my tights off slowly. His eyes are low as he takes in my nearly-naked body. All that's left are my thin, black underwear clinging to my wet lips.

Max's eyes flick up to mine, and he shakes his head slowly. He takes a deep breath, running his fingers gently over my hips.

"You're so fucking perfect, Naomi."

I roll my hips towards him as I bite my lip. He groans again, peeling my underwear off, sliding it inch by inch down my legs.

The heat is making my cheeks burn. I can only imagine how red they are.

But Max doesn't seem to care. He leans his body down and kisses me again, swiping his tongue across mine and groaning as my lips part. He reaches between my legs and moans when he feels my wetness.

My head is spinning. The instant his hand touches my slit, my whole body shivers. He presses his chest against mine, working his fingers ever so gently back and forth until they're as wet as I am.

"You like that?" He growls in my ear.

"Yes," I gasp as his finger twirls over my bud. *Yes* doesn't even begin to cover it. It's like a sensory overload. His scent is filling my nostrils, and the weight of his chest against mine is making my head spin. I can't even tell what he's doing with his fingers, because it just feels like one hot ball of pleasure between my legs.

It feels like I'm going to explode.

I reach down towards his boxers and gasp when I feel his throbbing erection. When he was carrying me, I thought it was big. Feeling it in my hand is something else altogether. Max's breath gets heavier as I touch him. He pushes his boxers down his legs and kicks them away.

I wrap my hand around his hardness and he groans. He stays there for a moment, unmoving, as I work my hand up and down his shaft.

Then, as if he remembers himself, he starts touching me again. His touch is faster, more insistent. He rolls my clit between his fingers as I stroke him. His breath is short and hot as it washes over my shoulder. He groans as his hot erection throbs in my hand, and then he pulls my hand away.

"Stop," he growls. "Not yet. Not like that."

Before I can protest, he crushes his lips against mine and kicks my legs apart. With his hands, he holds my thighs wide and moves down between them, glancing up at me only once before diving his head between my legs.

When his tongue touches my slit, my body arches. I gasp, tangling my fingers into his hair. I lean into the pleasure. Squeezing my eyes shut, I bite my lip and let the waves of warmth and ecstasy wash over me with every flick of his tongue.

He groans, glancing up at me. "You taste so good," he growls, and a flicker of heat flashes through me. The thought of him enjoying what he's doing is almost too much for me to process. His hands run over my stomach and he dips his head back down between my legs with a moan.

Every time his tongue twirls around my bud, he urges me closer to orgasm. When his fingers slip inside me, my body contracts around them and I know I'm past the point of no return. It only takes a few more seconds, a few more touches, a few more noises, and I'm flying over the edge.

I squeeze my legs around his head and arch my back as my orgasm explodes. Wave after wave of pleasure crashes into me until I'm screaming Max's name. I tangle my fingers into his hair and roll my hips towards him, gasping with every new sensation.

He holds me down. His tongue doesn't stop and his hands keep moving until my body has quieted down. The only movement between us is the soft kiss he lays on my mound and the heaving of my chest. Little thrills pass through my body as I try to recover.

Finally, Max lifts himself up and comes to lay beside me. I can see his shaft, hard as rock, throbbing against his belly when I turn towards him. He lays a heavy, muscled arm across my body and chuckles.

"You liked that?"

"It was okay," I grin.

"Just okay?" His eyebrow quirks.

"Maybe a bit better than okay," I laugh, and he pulls me in for a kiss.

25

MAX

I'VE BEEN THINKING of Naomi like this for a long time, but reality is so, so much better than my imagination. I can still taste her on my lips when she rolls towards me. Running my hands up her sides, I brush my fingertips along the edge of her breast and watch her shiver.

"I like making you come," I growl.

Her eyes flutter open and she looks at me, grinning. "Well that's lucky for me."

"I'm the lucky one."

I kiss her again, letting her taste her own juices on my lips. My whole body is vibrating. I'm harder than I've ever been, and every time she moves or moans or touches me, I feel like I'm going to explode. I'm like a tightly wound spring, and I don't know what's going to set me off.

She moves closer to me, running her soft hands up my chest. My bronzed skin makes her arm look like porcelain. She rests her head on the pillow and I lean over to kiss the spattering of freckles across her nose.

She smiles and runs her fingers through my hair. Then, her eyes flash and she moves her hand lower. My heart thumps. When she wraps her delicate fingers around my girth, I groan.

This is heaven.

It has to be. How else could I explain it? It feels too good to be true. It's like I'm drunk off her touch. My head is spinning and my heart is hammering against my ribcage. She moves her body closer to mine, pressing her skin against me. I inhale deeply, filling my nose with her scent.

It only takes a moment for me to get a condom from the nightstand. Naomi sits up, stradling my hips, and rolls it down over my shaft. Her emerald eyes flick up towards me, and she bites her lip seductively. Does she even realize how good she looks right now?

My eyes run down her body until I see what she's doing with her hands. She positions her hips above me, gasping gently as the tip of my cock brushes her slit.

Then, she sits down on top of me.

It's like an out of body experience. I watch her mouth drop open as she moans, her head falling backwards she sinks down on top of me, rolling her hips to accept every hard inch of me. I groan with her, my hands on her hips pulling her down deeper. When I'm sheathed to the hilt, she opens her eyes and places her hands on my chest.

Her breaths are short as she opens her eyes wider, moving her hips on top of me. I moan again, wrapping my hands around her hips and pulling her on top of me. Her fingers curl into my chest and I lift my head, watching as she rides me.

From there, I lose control. It feels too good. I can't think straight, can't breathe, can't do anything except roll my hips towards her over and over as she bounces on top of me. Her hair falls around her shoulders like a mane as her mouth falls open.

She looks like a fucking angel.

My angel.

My hand flies to her cheek and I pull her down for a kiss. She falls on top of me, her mouth devouring mine as her body opens up for me. I push myself deeper inside her, groaning as she shifts to take *all* of me. I wrap my arms around her tighter.

It's her moan that sends me over the edge. Her whole body shivers and I feel her contract around my shaft, and then her back arches. She screams, throwing her head back with her eyes squeezed shut.

"That's it," I groan, pulling her hips down on top of me. "Come on my cock."

My words seem to spur her on. She pants in my ear, riding the waves of pleasure that I can see crashing into her.

Fuck, I love making this woman orgasm.

I can't hold back any more. I explode. Her walls contract around me, milking me until I fill the condom. I shudder, shivering and convulsing as my fingers sink into her flesh. She's breathing heavily, her skin sticky with sweat and pleasure as we finally relax.

I run my fingers up her spine, gently brushing her skin. She shivers. Groaning, she slides off me and rolls onto her back. She throws her arm over her eyes and I watch her chest heave up and down as she gulps in air. I take off the used condom and get up to toss it in the trash, grabbing a towel from the chair.

When I slide back in bed, I hand Naomi the towel. She takes it, throwing it over her body and shaking her head.

"That was nice," she whispers. It's almost as if she can't get her voice to work properly.

I chuckle. "It was."

I wrap my arms around her and pull her in for another

kiss. We lay there until we fall asleep in each other's arms. My sleep is deep, dreamless and peaceful.

FROM THAT DAY ON, Naomi spends most evenings at my place. We don't talk about our previous conversation, about keeping this strictly business. It's like a dam has broken, and all we can do is hold on to each other for dear life. I look forward to coming home from work and calling her. We make dinner, we watch movies, we do everything and nothing together.

My parents go back to their house in the Sands Point, satisfied that I've found my match. As the days pass, I start to think that I've found her too.

I ignore the doubt in my heart. Once in a while, it whispers in my ear: would Naomi be here if we didn't have a contract?

ONE EVENING, Naomi sits on my sofa and pulls out her work notes. She sits with her legs folded underneath her, chewing the end of her pen. I glance over her shoulder, watching her scratch down notes for tomorrow's clients. She looks up at me, smiling as I lean down to lay a soft kiss on her lips.

"I should probably get going," she says. "Early start."

"Spend the night," I say, resting my hands on her shoulders. I massage them gently as she moans, closing her eyes and leaning her head to one side.

"I don't have any clothes for work," she says.

"Bring some here. I'll get you a toothbrush. You're here most evenings anyway, it doesn't make sense for you to go home every night. It's faster to get to work from here."

She takes a deep breath, and I lay a kiss on the top of her head.

"I want to wake up next to you," I say, brushing my cheek against hers. She turns and lays a kiss on my lips, and then laughs.

"Well I'm here all the time anyway," she says. "Might as well bring a change of underwear."

"I'll clear a drawer for you," I grin. "Want to go grab some stuff at your place tonight?"

Her eyes spark and she nods her chin gently. "Sure," she says, and my heart thumps.

26

NAOMI

AFTER THE EXCITEMENT of our first few days as an 'engaged' couple, life with Max becomes somewhat normal. We're almost like a real couple.

Well, I guess we *are* a real couple. I sleep over at his place —he doesn't come to mine so much, since mine is smaller and further away from both our workplaces. We go on dates, we watch Netflix and movies in the evenings.

There's still a little voice in my head that says 'this is a bad idea'. Besides the obvious—what happens when the month is over?—there's so many things that could go wrong. What if someone finds out? What if his parents catch on? What if my mom finds out?

What if Max changes his mind?

Is any of this *real*? He's paid me so much money, but I try not to think about that. It doesn't seem to bother him at all. He never mentions it once the contract is signed and the money has been paid. After a little while, I stop thinking about it, too.

Once his parents leave, the media attention dies down and we just live our lives.

. . .

ABOUT A WEEK after my mother's surprise visit, she calls me while I'm at Max's to tell me she'll be in the city and she wants to meet Max. I sigh, knowing that I won't be able to get out of it. She may not approve of weddings, or marriages, or *me* getting married, but she'll still want to meet a guy I'm supposed to be engaged to.

I get off the phone and look over at Max as he stands in the kitchen. His eyebrow is arched. He grabs a hot tortilla and places it on a plate for me, nodding to the skillet full of chicken.

"What's going on? Fajitas are ready."

"They smell delicious," I say, jumping up. "I never knew you were such a good cook."

"Was that your mom on the phone? How is she doing?"

"She's doing pretty well," I say, spooning some chicken onto my tortilla. I can feel Max's eyes on me, but I ignore him. Instead, I focus on the cheese and salsa for my fajita. Priorities, right?

"Sounded like she wanted something," he prompts.

I chuckle. "She wants to meet you, actually." I keep my eyes on my food. I can feel his gaze on me, and I finally drag my eyes over to him.

"You don't seem too happy about that," he grins.

"Are you?"

"Well, you *are* my fiancée."

"Fake fiancée."

"And you've met my parents, so it's only fair that I would meet yours, too."

My heart thumps and his eyes flash. I shake my head, finally letting myself laugh.

"You're enjoying this, aren't you?"

"What?" He says, turning to his own tortilla. It's his turn to focus on the chicken as his lips twitch into a grin.

"You're enjoying torturing me like this," I laugh.

"Torture!"

"Yes, torture," I say, wrapping my arms around his waist. "This was all just some elaborate ploy to get me to go out with you."

"You caught me," he laughs. He wraps his arms around me and presses his lips to mine. "I'd love to meet your mom. She sounds amazing. Just like you."

"Smooth talker," I laugh. A blush stains my cheeks as my heart does a backflip. Just like every other time he's around.

So much for keeping things professional.

This is starting to feel way, way too real. But I'm not sure I'm mad about that. I don't know how I feel, except that I'm happier with Max than I've been in a long time.

We eat our fajitas, and then I call my mother back. Max agrees to have her over at his place for dinner. I wrap my arms around his neck and kiss him gently. His tall, muscular frame feels so solid against me. He growls and I feel it vibrate through my chest, and he pulls me in with a grin.

We leave the dishes in the sink for a while—we've got better things to do.

THE NEXT DAY, I meet my mom at the entrance to Max's apartment building. I try to keep my face neutral, but I can't believe how much she's changed in only a couple weeks. Thick, black bags mar the skin under her eyes, and her skin has a sallow, yellow color.

When she smiles, her skin stretches and wrinkles around her mouth and her eyes still sparkle with their old energy. She wraps her arms around me.

"You feel thin, Mom," I say. "Have you lost weight?"

"These treatments make me lose my appetite," she says. "It's only been a couple weeks, but the thought of doing this for seven more weeks is a bit daunting."

"Are you driving all the way here an all the way back every time you have an appointment?"

"What else would I do?" She laughs as I lead her towards the elevator. I press the button for the top floor and the doors open right away.

"Why don't you stay at my place. I can stay with Max, so you'll have the whole apartment to yourself. Just until this round of treatments are over."

She smiles sadly, brushing the back of her hand over my cheek. "You're so sweet, Naomi. You know I hate the city."

"I don't like you driving so much. Didn't you say the nausea is getting worse?"

"I'm a grown woman," my mother laughs. "I've taken care of myself for a lot longer than you have."

I squeeze my mom's hand as the elevator dings open and we step out onto Max's floor. "I know, but..." I sigh. "Just let me help you."

"I'm fine, honey."

We walk into the apartment, and Max stands to greet us.

"Jackie! Uh, Mrs. Rose!" He smiles at my mother, taking a hesitant step forward as if he's going to hug her. He reconsiders, sticking his hand out and nodding his chin.

My mom laughs.

Cute.

She swats his hand away and wraps her arms around his thick torso. Her head barely gets halfway up his chest, and she looks tiny and frail in his arms. He hugs her awkwardly, stepping back and clearing his throat.

"I made a roast chicken," he proclaims, gesturing towards the oven. Mom glances at me, grinning.

"Sounds lovely," my mom says. "And call me Jackie, please." She smiles at him and then winks at me. My shoulders relax and I let out a breath I didn't know I was holding.

By the time dinner is over, we've laughed and eaten until our stomachs are full and our eyelids are heavy. I notice my mother pushing the food around her plate as she eats even more slowly than usual. She looks absolutely exhausted. Max exchanges a glance with me, and clears his throat.

"Why don't you stay at Naomi's place tonight? I can drive you there, Naomi can follow with your car. Then if you want, you can head back to the country in the morning."

My mom yawns, glancing at me and shaking her head. "Fine," she laughs. "You've convinced me. I can't see far enough to walk to your front door, let alone drive for two hours."

I breathe a sigh of relief, smiling at Max as my heart grows in my chest. He read my mind—he's considerate enough to realize what my mom is going through and is willing to help.

We drive Mom to my place and settle her in, and then I get into the passenger's seat of Max's car. I rest my head on his shoulder as we drive back to his place.

"My mom likes you," I say as my eyes start to close.

"Yeah?"

"Yeah."

"Good," he says, leaning his cheek against the top of my head. "I was nervous."

I chuckle, taking a deep breath and lifting my head off his shoulder. I glance at Max's face as heat spreads across my chest. I'm not used to all these feelings. It's overwhelming and confusing, but it's also *nice*. My hand finds his, and I give it a squeeze.

Tonight felt very real. Maybe the more we *say* we're getting married, the more it feels like we will. What happens when this month is up?

Max squeezes my hand back, smiling at me. His eyes are soft and tender, and he looks at me for a long moment before turning back to the road. He lifts my fingers up to his mouth and kisses them softly as I lean back against the head rest.

27
MAX

BEFORE I KNOW IT, the month is up. I wake up on the morning of the last contracted day of our agreement and turn around in bed to see Naomi sleeping. I brush a strand of hair off her face. She groans, shifting over towards me and laying her cheek on my chest. I wrap my arm around her and sigh, staring at the ceiling.

I'm not ready for this to be over.

I'm not ready to wake up on my own, or to tell the world that Naomi and I aren't together anymore. Over the past couple weeks, this has felt very, very real.

Too real.

It feels normal to call her my fiancée. It feels normal to hold her hand in public, and to kiss her temple. Going out on dates isn't an act—I really do like getting to know her. I love spending time with her. I love waking up to her in bed beside me.

She takes a deep breath and opens her eyes, looking up at me and smiling.

"Morning," she says.

"Morning, beautiful."

I kiss her forehead, and she snuggles into me.

"You okay?" She asks, looking up at me again. She runs her fingers back and forth across my chest.

"Yeah, why?" I answer. How did she know I was upset?

"You seem tense."

I swallow. "Today's the last day of the contract," I answer. She leans her cheek against my chest again and her fingers stop moving.

"Oh," she says. "That went by quickly. I hadn't realized it had been a month already."

"Will you... I want... would you consider renewing the contract for another month?"

She stiffens, and then turns to look at me. Her eyes are wide and she swallows, rolling over onto her back and slipping her hand into mine.

"Yes," she replies slowly. "But I just... It feels wrong to take your money."

"I think it's best if we stick to the contract. I know you were worried about things getting messy, but the easiest way is to just go forward with it. It'll get messier if we don't stick with the terms. Both of us, I mean. No matter what is going on between us. Trust me," I say. "The money isn't a big deal."

"Maybe not to you," she says with a strangled voice. "But to me and my mom it is."

My chest squeezes. *Damn it.*

"I know, I didn't mean it like that. I just meant that—"

"It's okay. I get it. I'll take your money," she says, swinging her legs over the edge of the bed and standing up. My eyes drift down to her bare ass and a blade of heat passes through me.

I know she's upset, but I can't help how my body reacts to the sight of her. She rubs her arms with her hands, shivering.

Then, she shrugs into a bathrobe, still not turning to look at me.

"Are you okay?"

"I'm fine."

Uh-oh.

"Naomi?"

"I'm fine, Max," she says. "I need to get to work."

"I don't understand, I thought that you'd be happy to be getting more money. I don't—"

"It's not just about money, Max," she says, finally looking me in the eye. "But I'll take your money. I don't really have the luxury of saying no." She sighs, grabbing a towel from the chair and draping it over her arm. Her cheeks are flushed and her hair is messy, but her eyes are bright when she looks at me.

"This is just a really confusing situation. I don't know what's real and what isn't."

I stand up out of bed, walking to her and wrapping my arms around her. I pull her close, running my thumb over her pout and tilting her chin up.

"I'm not pretending."

"So why go on with this stupid contract? I mean, it's not stupid. And we're not actually engaged, and of course I need the money, I just..."

She takes a deep breath.

"I don't know. I don't know anything."

I chuckle, pulling her closer to me. "Naomi," I say gently. She lifts her eyes up to me and a bolt of lightening passes through my chest. "This is real," I say. It comes out as a whisper. My heartbeat is roaring in my ears and I can hardly hear myself speak.

Her mouth drops open and she nods, her eyes filling with tears.

"It is?"

"Isn't it?"

She starts laughing, shaking her head and pulling away from me. "We are the worst at communicating," she laughs. "How about you just give me a shitload of money and I'll keep pretending to be your fiancée and we can keep dating—or whatever—and then we can revisit this in another month."

A grin spreads over my lips and I nod. "Deal."

BY THE TIME we're both ready for work, the awkwardness has passed. I kiss her goodbye on the sidewalk in front of my building.

"I'm taking my mom to her treatment tonight, so I'll be home a bit late," she says. Her mom has ended up staying at her apartment full-time, and I'm enjoying Naomi staying at my place. At first, we justified it as keeping up appearances of being engaged, but I think both of us just wanted to spend the time together.

I nod. "Sounds good." I kiss her again. "See you tonight."

"Love you," she says as she starts to turn away, and then her eyes widen. "I mean. God. Sorry. I don't... I didn't... Shit." She shakes her head, staring at the sidewalk next to my foot. "This is what I mean by things being confusing! How am I supposed to pretend to be in love with you all the time in public? And then we act like we're together in private and I just don't know what I'm supposed to say, and—"

She only stops talking when I crush my lips against hers. I can feel her pulse hammering as hard as mine is. She wraps her arms around my neck and kisses me feverishly until we pull away, panting. I rest my forehead against hers, swaying gently from side to side.

"I told you, Naomi. This is real." I kiss the tip of her nose. "I think... I love you too."

"Oh," she says, and then she bites her lip and smiles. "Okay. So I'll see you tonight?"

"See you tonight."

I watch her walk away before getting into my car. I can't keep the smile from my face until I get to the office and see my father waiting for me. He's sitting in my office, his fingers tented in front of his chest as he waits for me.

I drop my briefcase on my desk and nod to him. "Hello," I say. "To what do I owe the honor? I didn't know you were in town. How's the acquisition going?"

"The acquisition is on track, and the board has approved you as the new director of the international division." He says curtly.

I sit down, waving my assistant away as she pokes her head through the door. She closes it softly and I turn my attention back to my dad.

"So that's a good thing," I respond. It almost sounds like a question. The way my father's face looks, it doesn't seem like a good thing at all.

He sighs, pulling a folder out of his briefcase and placing it on my desk.

"It would be a good thing, except for that."

"What's this?" I flip the folder open.

"Your little fiancée isn't who she says she is."

My stomach drops like a rock, and once again my pulse is thundering in my ears. This time, it's not from happiness, though. I feel like I might throw up.

I look at my father. His lips are set in a thin, grim line, and his eyebrows are drawn together. He takes a deep breath and shakes his head.

"I'm sorry, son," he says. "I could tell you liked her."

28

NAOMI

"How's Maxie doing these days?" My mom says as the nurse hooks her up to the IV. I sit back in my chair, glancing at my phone's blank screen. I frown before putting it away. I haven't heard from Max all day, which is unusual.

Typically he'd text me at least once during the day—even just a funny picture or a couple words about his day. I've sent him a message and he hasn't replied yet.

Was he freaked out by the whole 'I love you' thing?

I know I am, kind of. It just blurted out of me, I couldn't help it.

He's probably just busy.

My mother is staring at me expectantly, so I force a smile on my face. "Call him Max, please, Mom," I laugh. "Maxie sounds like maxi-pad."

"I'll call him whatever I want to call him," she huffs as she watches the nurse hook her up to a bag of medication. "Thank you, Cheryl. You found a vein easily today, didn't you?"

"You're nice and veiny, Jackie," the nurse laughs. "We all fight to be the ones to hook you up." She gestures to the other nurses and my mother smiles proudly, smoothing her hands on her lap. She leans back in her chair, breathing deeply and looking at me.

"You never answered my question. How's Max doing?"

"He's good," I say. "Busy with work, as usual. Him and his football buddies are going to go to the game on Sunday."

"That will be nice," she replies. I put my hand over hers, stroking it gently. Her skin is paper-thin, and I hate how sunken her cheeks are. At least she doesn't have to drive for hours to get here anymore.

I sit with her until the treatment is over, and then I help her into the wheelchair.

"It's so silly that I have to do this. I can walk!"

"Hospital policy," I say. "Just enjoy the ride." We walk in silence towards the exit. "I noticed you got some art supplies," I say. "Have you been painting?"

"Yes, but you can't peek at it," my mom says, reaching up and squeezing my hand on the wheelchair. "It's a wedding present for you and Maxie."

A dagger slides into my heart.

It's one thing for Max and I to be confused. It's another thing entirely to be getting my Mom's hopes up. A wedding present? I didn't think she'd be happy with me getting married at all.

"You've always told me to never get married. What's going on?"

"Maybe my brush with mortality is making me sentimental," she says, and I can hear the grin in her voice. Then she sighs and turns her head to try to look at me as I push her down the stark white hospital hallways. "I'm happy for you, Naomi. Max is wonderful."

I swallow past the lump in my throat, nodding.

"Yeah," I say. "He is."

. . .

By the time my mom is back at my apartment, I check my phone for what feels like the thousandth time. Still nothing from Max. I dial his number on my way out and frown when it goes straight to voicemail.

This definitely isn't normal.

Has something happened to him? I don't have any of his friends' phone numbers, and it would probably be a bit of an overreaction to call them when I haven't heard from him in a couple hours.

Instead, I just get in my car and head towards his place. I'm sure he'll be there, greeting me with a big hug and a kiss. Still, a niggling feeling at the base of my skull makes me uneasy. Something doesn't feel right.

I check my phone again. I go into my social media applications, and see that he's online. I send him a quick message.

He sees it, but doesn't answer.

My heart thumps.

What's going on?

Maybe saying the 'L' word really did freak him out this morning. Am I going to go home to a serious 'talk'? What am I walking into?

I resist the urge to send another message. Is he mad at me?

My hands are shaking. I take a deep breath. My mind is going into a panic vortex, and I need to just stop worrying. Max is fine, we're fine, I'll go home and everything will be okay.

I dial Ariana's number and put her on through the car's hands-free setting.

"Well hello, stranger," she says as she answers. "Long time no talk."

"I know," I say. "I'm sorry."

"No, no, no, I get it," she laughs. "You're all shacked up with a multi-billionaire, or whatever. You don't have time for your friends anymore. If you didn't work with Meg, you probably wouldn't talk to her at all."

"Stop it," I laugh. "What's new with you? Any new boyfriends?"

Ariana laughs. "Always." She launches into a story about her newest beau, an investment banker who works on Wall Street.

"He booked a penthouse suite at the Ritz. It was *insane*. He wants to fly me out to Paris!"

"No," I laugh. "Really?!"

"Romantic getaway," she laughs.

"Are you going to do it?"

"Are you joking? Obviously!"

I laugh and the tightness in my chest eases. Ariana's right, I've been neglecting my friends too much. Max could be busy, or cooking, or he could be doing a thousand things that stop him from answering my text. I shouldn't freak out.

By the time I hang up the phone, I feel better.

I park under Max's building and head towards the elevator, taking a deep breath and smiling. I'll wrap my arms around Max, around my *love*, and I'll kiss his gorgeous lips.

Life is *good*, and I shouldn't freak myself out over nothing.

When I get to the door, I take a deep breath. I push it open, step through and call out as I walk in.

"Hello? I'm home!"

I don't see Max until he appears from the bedroom door. I freeze. His eyes are sunken. They're darker than I've ever seen them, as black as the ocean during a storm. His mouth is turned down, with lines carved across his forehead. His arms hang loosely by his side. He clenches and unclenches his fists.

I clutch my purse, frowning.

"Max," I say. "What's wrong?"

My pulse is thundering. He opens his mouth and then closes it again. His eyebrows draw together another fraction of an inch, and another line appears on his forehead. He lets out a sigh, shaking his head slowly.

"What?" I say. I take a step forward. "What's going on? What happened? Is everything okay?"

"No," he finally says. His voice is strangled. I hardly recognize it. There's none of the warmth, none of the familiarity that I'm used to. His eyes flash and his mouth turns down. "No, everything is most definitely not 'okay'."

He spits out the last word, and my entire world crumbles around me.

29

MAX

I CLOSE my fists to stop my hands from shaking. My whole body is stiff with tension. Naomi's eyes are wide. Her eyebrows draw together as she takes a step towards me.

"Don't—" I almost yell. I stick my hand out in front of me and Naomi stops. I take a deep, trembling breath. "Stay right there."

"What's going on, Max?"

"Oh, stop pretending," I spit. "I know everything." The burning in my chest hasn't stopped since I read her file. The whole afternoon, I've gone over it, and over it, and over it, but I still can hardly believe that she's lied to me like this.

"What's that supposed to mean?"

"Stop playing dumb!" The words rip my throat apart. My nails dig in to my palms so hard that I wonder if they might bleed. I watch Naomi's throat move as she swallows. She's clutching her purse close to her body, her green eyes staring at me in shock.

I take a deep breath.

"My parents hired a private investigator."

Her eyes widen some more. I don't know if it's genuine

shock, or fear of being found out, or just another act on her part.

"Yeah," I spit. "And he found out some very interesting things."

"Like what?" Her voice is small, and her knuckles are white where they clutch her purse strap.

"Still not going to admit it, hey?"

"Max, I have no idea what you're talking about." Her voice is gentle, and her eyes fill with concern. "This morning—"

"This morning means nothing," I say, turning my head away from her. It hurts to look at her, to hear her. I don't want to get close enough to smell the sweet scent that clings to her. I lean my palms on the kitchen counter as I drag another long breath into my lungs.

When she says nothing, I turn to look at her. Her lip is trembling, and her eyes are filling with tears. My heart shatters, and black anger fills up the void where my heart used to be.

Still, *still* she denies it!

I scoff, shaking my head.

"I found out about your father, Naomi. The gig is up."

Naomi's jaw drops. A tear spills out of her eye and she takes a step forward before stopping herself. When she speaks, her voice is nothing more than a hoarse whisper.

"My father? You found out—what did you find out?"

Her breath is short and her eyes are desperate. I laugh bitterly, shaking my head.

"Just stop, Naomi. Look, at least this gave us an excuse to end this stupid fake engagement. Right on time, too."

She makes a strangled noise and takes a trembling breath.

"What did you find out?" She whispers. "Who is my father?"

Doubt pierces my chest at the desperation in her words. I thought she would deny everything, that she would say she hadn't nothing to do with her father—but to deny knowing him entirely?

Tears are streaming down her face and she takes another step towards me.

"Please, Max." Her voice is stronger. "Please. Who is he? Just give me a name."

Doubt and love battle against the anger and betrayal that have filled my chest. Watching her crying makes my entire body ache. Knowing that she betrayed me, lied to me—is probably *still* lying to me—that's a dagger straight through my heart.

I snarl. "Cut the bullshit, Naomi. You know your father was selling his company to mine, and he wanted to keep control of it, so he set you onto me. This whole thing—it was all an act. You were just a pawn in this business deal, and you know it."

"'Set me onto you'?" She says, laughing as she cries. "Are you fucking kidding me? This engagement was *your* idea."

She shakes her head, moving her hand to her chest and opening her mouth. Her other hand flies to her lips, and she stares at the ground.

"I don't know how you did it, but you did."

Tears drop from her chin onto the carpet until she looks at me again.

"I never met my father. My mother is an artist. I am a physical therapist. I used the money you gave me to pay for her chemotherapy. If she needs to have a mastectomy, I'll pay for that too. That's where the rest of the money will go. If not, I'll use it to pay off the sixty thousand dollars in student debt I have. Did your fucking private investigator find out about that?"

"Oh, don't play the cancer card, Naomi."

Her face twists. "The 'cancer card'? Listen to yourself, Max." She shakes her head. "Or maybe I should have known. I should have known that it was too good to be true. I should have known that the stories about you were based on fact. Maybe the tabloids were right about you."

She stands up straighter, wiping her cheeks with her palms. Her lower lip is still trembling, but she shakes her head from side to side. She takes a deep breath, closing her eyes for a moment and then staring at me with those sharp, green eyes that I thought I loved.

"What's his name, Max? What's my father's name?"

"Get out of my house. Your stuff is in the bag," I say, waving to the black garbage bag I filled with her things. It was the first thing I did when I got home, when the anger was fresh and raw. She glances at the bag and then back at me.

"Please, Max. Tell me." Her face crumples again and it feels like the a twist of a dagger in my heart. Alarm bells ring in my head. It seems so *real*. She really wants to know his name.

But if I answer, if I tell her his name, isn't that admitting that I believe her? She already *knows* her father's name! She's been acting at her father's request all this time!

The only reason that Naomi and I are in this mess is because somehow—I'm not sure how, but *somehow*, she and her father planned it. He knew that once my parents acquired his company, he would lose everything he worked for. He found out that I'd be the director of the new division, and he didn't want to let it go.

The acquisition isn't as amicable as it seemed at the golf center. I can still remember the way Jerry's eyes flashed when he shook my hand. I thought the chill that went down my spine was just because my father was forcing me to get married.

Naomi is still staring at me, and a thought enters my head uninvited: maybe I'm remembering things wrong. Maybe I'm making up that whole chill down my spine. Maybe her father knew I'd be in charge, and he was just sizing me up. Like all my father's business associates do.

I'm frozen. I'm stuck. If I agree with Naomi, I admit that I was wrong.

I'm not ready to do that. I don't trust her—it's too confusing. It's too much of a coincidence.

But if I don't agree with her, then she leaves forever. Whatever we had together is done.

My lips press together and I turn away from her. What we had wasn't real. It was all fake. It was all some ploy to play me and my father, and I don't owe anything to her. I walk towards the big glass wall at the other end of the apartment, turning my back on Naomi. I cross my arms over my chest and grind my teeth together.

She sniffles, and then a plastic bag rustles. It's not until I hear the door close that I glance over my shoulder.

She's gone.

I sink down onto the couch and rub my hands over my face.

It's over.

30

NAOMI

I slide into my car and put the bag of clothes on the passenger's seat beside me. I close the door and put the keys in the ignition, but I don't turn the car on. I just sit there, with my hands on the steering wheel as I stare out into nothing.

What just happened?

Did we just break up?

He knows who my father is!

He knows who my father is and he wouldn't tell me. My chest feels like there's a huge hand squeezing it tight. It's hard to breathe. My lungs just can't get enough air. I put a hand to my heart, closing my eyes to try to take a deep breath.

I replay everything that just happened over and over to try to make sense of it.

But I can't.

None of it makes sense.

How could he think that I planned this? Does he think my mother's illness is fake? Does he think that I somehow convinced *him* to convince *me* to marry him? This whole thing is crazy! How could he think that? It makes no sense!

Another question needles at my brain. It's the same question that's plagued me my entire life.

Who is my father?

Max *knows*, and he refuses to tell me. I saw the vindictive curl of his lip when I asked. He turned away from me. He wouldn't even say the name. I've lost Max, lost whatever we had, and I can't even find out who Max thinks is behind it all.

My hands tighten on the steering wheel, and I rest my forehead against them. I squeeze my eyes shut, clenching my jaw and taking long, slow breaths in and out of my nose.

Through all the confusion, and all the questions, one emotion underpins everything: pure, unblemished heartbreak. I told him I loved him this morning, and it was true. I was starting to think that being engaged to him was a good idea. I was starting to think that maybe this could *work*.

How stupid could I be?

Of course this whole thing was going to blow up in my face.

I *knew* it would, and I still went through with it. I still convinced myself that developing feelings for Max wasn't a problem.

Loving him was the fuel that made this whole thing detonate.

The hand squeezing my chest tightens, and I sit up straighter. I lean my head against the headrest, sucking air in through my nose and trying to stop the tears from falling down my face.

I'm sick of crying.

What did I expect? That we would live happily ever after? That he would decide to get rid of the contract and marry me for me?

Stupid, stupid girl.

A sob shudders through me, and I keep my eyes closed as

tears spill out of them. My knuckles are white as I clutch the steering wheel. When I take one off and reach into my purse, I can hardly stop myself from shaking. I dial my mom's phone number, and then hang up right away.

I stare at the blank screen, seeing my tear-stained reflection in it.

I can't call my mother. She's just had a brutal chemotherapy appointment. She's probably asleep by now, or too nauseous to deal with my sorry, heartbroken ass.

What would I tell her? Sorry mom, I lied. I'm not engaged, but I accidentally fell in love with the man I was pretending to be in love with and he broke my heart.

Maybe I deserve it for being so fucking stupid.

Instead, I dial Meg's number. As soon as she answers, I sob incoherently.

"Whoa, whoa, Naomi, is everything okay?"

"No," I wail. "It's not okay. Max broke up with me and he thinks that I set the whole thing up but I didn't, I don't even know who my dad is!" I snort, my breath shaking as I cry into the phone.

"Okay, slow down Naomi, come on. Are you safe right now? Do you need me to come get you?"

"No," I cry. "Can I sleep at your place?"

"Of course," she says. "I'll boil some water for tea."

"You got anything stronger?"

Meg chuckles. "That bad, hey?"

"Yeah."

"You okay to drive?"

"Yeah. See you soon."

When I hang up the phone, I take a deep breath. The air burns my lungs, and I swallow past a huge lump in my throat. I turn the key in the ignition and glance out the window at

Max's building. I turn to the plastic bag stuffed with clothes, and I wipe my eyes one more time.

"Goodbye, Max," I whisper, and then I pull out into the street and drive to Meg's house.

SHE GREETS me with a hug and a bottle of wine. I laugh as the tears well in my eyes again, and she wraps me in her arms again without saying anything.

Half a bottle of wine and a full box of tissues later, I've told her everything from the accidental 'I love you' to the final goodbye.

She takes a deep breath.

"Wow."

"I know."

"So he thinks that you masterminded this whole thing?"

I nod.

"And he thinks that you pretended about not knowing your father and you wanted to somehow retain control of this... this merger or whatever?"

"He called it an acquisition."

"Whatever," she says, swirling her wine in her glass. She shakes her head. "Honey, he sounds like a fucking moron." I snort-laugh. "How could he believe those things? Does he know your mom has freaking *cancer*? Does he think you're faking that too? Does he think you rented a shitty apartment just to make your master plan more believable?"

"I don't know," I say, grinning through my tears. "I don't get it."

"Maybe he's just hurting, and he'll come around."

"I'm not sure I want that. I mean, if he won't even hear me out when he thinks something like this happens, then is he really worth it? What if we got in a fight about something real?"

Meg purses her lips and I shake my head.

"Don't say it."

"What?" Her eyebrows shoot up.

"Just don't."

"I don't know what you're talking about."

"I know you're dying to say 'I told you so'. I can see it in your face."

Meg's eyes flash, and a grin spreads across her lips. She takes a sip of wine and shakes her head. "I would never gloat over something like this."

"Oh, please," I laugh.

Meg shrugs.

"*Fine.*" I say before gulping down half my wine.

She turns to me, tilting her head and grinning. "Fine, what?"

"You can say it. But only *once.*"

Meg takes a deep breath, swirling her wine and shaking her head. "I always said he was trouble. Didn't I say that before this whole thing even started?"

She turns to me and smiles, throwing her arm across my shoulders and laughing.

"I'm joking, Naomi," she sighs. "Even *I* didn't see this coming. When I saw how happy you were, I thought this was the real deal."

I sniffle, and she squeezes me closer. She nods to the bottle.

"We've still got half a bottle to polish off."

"Don't worry, I won't let it go to waste."

She laughs, filling up my glass. We clink our glasses together, and then she looks at me with sadness in her eyes.

"In all honesty, Naomi, I'm sorry this happened."

"It's okay," I sigh.

"It's not. He's a bastard for not listening to you and for thinking you would do those things to him. Did he not get to know you at all? You're a fucking angel! And he's a double bastard for not even fucking telling you your father's name!"

"I think that's what bothers me the most. I *told* him how curious I was. I told him how much it had bothered me when I was a kid, and he still wouldn't tell me!"

"Maybe he thought that if he told you, it would be like admitting that he was wrong about the whole set-up conspiracy."

"Maybe," I say, and I smile sadly. "But hey... At least I got three hundred grand out of it."

"Atta girl," Meg grins. "Exactly."

"My mom's in treatment and her house won't go to fore-closure. And I might finally pay off my student loans."

"Who needs men when you have money? Squeeze 'em for every dirty red penny."

"Cheers to that," I laugh. But my heart aches and my eyes feel puffy. I'd rather have Max than his money, but it seems like that ship has sailed for good.

31

MAX

WHEN THE GREY light of dawn starts peeking through my blinds, I swing my legs over the side of the bed and stretch my neck from side to side.

I haven't slept at all. I tossed and turned all night, thinking of Naomi's face before she left. It was red, blotchy, and just as beautiful as always. Her eyes, though, they killed me. She looked as betrayed as I felt.

I did that to her. I made her feel that way. I'm the reason that she was in pain.

And for what?

Nothing makes sense. She's right—why would she lie about her mother? I've *seen* Jackie. I know she's sick. Was that just a coincidence that worked out well for their little plan?

I stand up, stalking to the living room and taking the private investigator's file out of my briefcase. I stare at the yellow folder, gritting my teeth and taking a deep breath.

I flick through it, reading everything carefully.

It's all there. Her mother's illness, the foreclosure on the house, her student loans. Why would she have financial troubles if her father owns a multi-million dollar corporation? Even if he was going through financial problems, which would explain the acquisition, he would still have had enough money to pay for her college fees ten years ago.

It just doesn't make sense.

Unless his company is in worse shape than he let on? Maybe that's why he wanted this sale. He just wants to get rid of his company before it goes under.

Another voice gets louder at the back of my mind. I ignore it, but it keeps saying the same thing over and over.

What if Naomi was telling the truth?

There are so many things that don't make sense. My parents pushing for the marriage, her initial refusal. Her mother's illness, her own financial troubles.

None of those things would be here if this was some master plan on the part of her father!

I shut the file, chucking it onto the couch and running my fingers through my hair. The sting of betrayal is raw in my chest. It feels exactly like it did when Farrah left me after my injury.

The ground has fallen away from under me, exactly how it did when I lost my football career, my girlfriend, and my entire future.

Once again, I'm a ship without rudder, being tossed around in the storm. I'm just hanging on for dear life.

And the only thing I can think of is Naomi. Her laugh, her eyes, her touch. The taste of her, the smell of her. The way she made me laugh, and the way my apartment felt like home whenever she was here.

She made me better.

She made me happy.

And now she's gone. I want to believe that she betrayed

me. The black hole in my heart wants to believe that she's just like the rest of them.

But is she?

I pull on a tee-shirt and jeans and throw on a jacket. I grab the file, shuffling through it for Jerry Irving's address. I need to talk to him. I need to hear it from his mouth, and look him in the eye when he denies it.

Man to man.

I ignore the voice that tells me Naomi's innocent in all this, and I focus on the burning anger in my chest. That's the only way I'll get to the bottom of this. I need to ignore my weaknesses, and focus on the truth, no matter how painful it might be.

Right now, seething, hot anger is giving me more strength than the thought that I've just lost the only woman I've ever truly loved.

I jump in my black Mercedes and punch in Jerry's office into my GPS. I glance at the clock—it's not even 7am yet. I sigh.

I need to go. I need to get out of my apartment and I need to get to the bottom of this. I put the car in gear and follow the GPS's metallic voice as she guides me through the streets. When I find the office building, I do a lap around the block and find somewhere to park.

The streets are still quiet. I take a deep breath and step out of my car. I spot a cafe near the entrance to the office building and check my watch.

Just after 7am.

I get myself a coffee, finding a seat near the window. My knee bounces up and down as I wait. I sip my coffee slowly, never taking my eyes off the entrance to Jerry's building.

It's nearly quarter to eight before I see Jerry walk in. He

checks his watch as he steps into the revolving door. I watch him disappear and my heart rate jumps.

My coffee is cold, but I still sit there for a few minutes and take another sip. It tastes bitter and burnt, but I hadn't noticed until now. The coffee shop is busier than it was when I walked in, with men and women in suits bustling in and out constantly.

I feel out of place in my old tee-shirt and unshaven face. I'm sure my face shows how little I slept last night, but none of that matters.

I take a deep breath. I'm not going to get any answers sitting here.

I chuck the rest of my cold coffee into the trash and walk towards the office building. The revolving doors suck me in, and I scan the wall for Jerry's company's name.

Irving, Co. Ltd. is on the seventeenth floor. I press the elevator button and glance over at the suit standing next to me. He's holding a coffee mug in one hand, and glances at an expensive watch on the other. The elevator dings open, and we step in together.

He looks me up and down before staring at his phone. I watch him scroll through dozens of emails as he tries his best to ignore me. He gets off on the twelfth floor, and I take a deep breath as I lean against the wall. It's unbearable to be so close to someone who looks that put together when I feel like I'm coming apart at the seams. When the doors open on the seventeenth floor, I'm greeted by a sleek glass partition and an all-white reception desk. I walk towards the pretty blonde receptionist and clear my throat.

"I'm here to see Jerry Irving."

"Is he expecting you?" She asks, looking me up and down.

"Just tell him Max Westbrook is here to see him." Her eyes widen slightly at my name, and she nods. She presses a few buttons on the phone and mutters into it, hanging it up and nodding to me.

"Follow me, please."

My heart thumps as we make our way down the hallway. It's lined with more glass offices and conference rooms. Nowhere to hide in Jerry's company. That's ironic, considering what he's just put Naomi up to.

Finally, at the far end of the building, the receptionist gestures to a door. The blinds are drawn and I can't see inside.

"Thanks," I say.

"He said to go on in."

I nod. She hovers for a moment, and then walks away. With a deep breath, I push open the door and step through.

Jerry's eyebrows shoot up when he sees me. I wish I'd worn a suit, or at least shaved this morning. I must look like hell.

"Max," he says, extending his hand. "To what do I owe the honor?"

I shake his hand and drop it as soon as I can. I resist the urge to wipe my hand on my pants. He gestures for me to sit. I lower myself stiffly as he does, his wide oak desk separating us.

"I'm here to talk about your daughter," I say.

His eyebrows shoot up and then draw together. He opens his mouth and shakes his head slightly.

"I'm sorry?"

"Your daughter, Naomi."

He clears his throat, staring at me. He glances down at my clothing once more, and his eyes fill with concern. "You must be mistaken, Max. I don't have a daughter."

Alarm bells start ringing in my head. What does he mean,

he doesn't have a daughter? The voice at the back of my mind is screaming at me—she was telling the truth.

But I'm not ready to believe it. He's bluffing.

"Cut the shit, Jerry. I know you set me up with her."

Jerry leans forward, splaying his hands on his desk.

"Max," he says. "I'm sorry, you've been misinformed. I don't have any kids."

32

NAOMI

I WAKE up on Meg's couch with swollen eyes and stiff limbs. I sigh, turning my head towards the window and squinting at the light. Meg is in the kitchen singing to herself. The smell of coffee wafts towards me, and I sit up like a groundhog poking its head out of its hole.

"Morning, sunshine," she says. "Coffee?"

"Please," I groan. It feels like I've been hit by a bus. I push myself off the couch and accept the steaming mug she hands me.

I slide into a kitchen chair and sigh.

"How are you feeling?"

"I'm supposed to have a physio appointment with Max today," I say.

She scoffs. "You think he'll show up?"

I laugh. "Not likely."

"That's the worst part of this whole thing. He was a good client. He was making good progress. Julia was talking about getting him to do a testimonial for the website. Big name client and all that."

"Well, I fucked that up, didn't I?"

She turns towards me, raising an eyebrow. "You didn't fuck anything up. You acted exactly how anyone would have, and then you were blindsided. Don't ever say that this is your fault."

I nod. "I might take a shower and then we can head to work, yeah?"

Meg smiles and nods. "Sure."

JULIA LOOKS at me when I walk in and gives me a pitying look that makes my stomach turn. I wonder how many people will look at me like that when they find out about me and Max? How many tabloid articles will talk about our split?

I never considered any of that when I agreed to pretend to be his fiancée.

"What's wrong, Naomi?" She asks, pulling me aside. "Is everything okay with your mom?"

"Everything's fine," I say. "I'm fine."

"You can take the day off if you need to," she says. She seems to have softened as a boss ever since she got engaged. Maybe love does that to a person—makes them soft. It sure did it to me.

I smile sadly. "As tempting as that is, I think I'd actually rather work."

"Okay. You'll tell me if you need anything?"

The way she's looking at me makes me want to punch something. Meg glances at me from the kitchen. She's pouring two cups of coffee, and all I want to do is smash the mug into a wall and scream into a pillow.

But I don't. I accept the coffee with a nod, and slink away to the furthest corner of the office.

All morning, I watch the clock.

Max's appointment is scheduled for 11am. I have three

clients between now and then, and I try my best to give them my undivided attention.

But all the while, the time is marching onwards, closer and closer to 11 o'clock.

"You okay, Naomi?" My long-time client, Daniel asks me. He came to me after a hip replacement surgery eight months ago. "You seem distracted."

I force a smile. "I'm fine, Daniel. Sorry about that. Now, let's get you over here on the exercise ball."

With renewed energy, I focus on my client. Once Daniel leaves, I'm once again staring at the clock. No clients from now until 11 o'clock—just a bit of paperwork to do. I slide behind my desk and write notes from the morning's appointments, pointedly ignoring the clock.

My heart starts beating faster when I raise my head and see it's almost time.

Is he going to show up?

Do I *want* him to show up?

The seconds tick by, and finally the clock strikes eleven. I glance at the door, palms sweaty and heart bouncing off my ribcage.

Nothing.

No movement. No Max.

I let out a sigh so loud that Meg looks over. She sees me glance away from the door, and gives me a sad smile. I wish she wouldn't pity me like that.

"Were you hoping he'd show up?"

"I don't know," I respond. "I'm relieved and disappointed at the same time. Is that possible?"

"You feel how you feel. It's all valid."

"This situation is so fucked up. I was so stupid to think that it would work out. What did I expect?"

"You made the best decisions with the hand you were

dealt, Naomi," Meg says gently. "Look at it this way, if you hadn't, your mother probably would have lost the house. She might not be getting the care she needs. You'd be in worse shape if that happened than because of some guy."

I know she's right, but her words sting. Max doesn't feel like 'some guy'. He doesn't feel like the kind of guy that's just a one-month fling. He doesn't feel like the kind of guy that I'll end up laughing about in a couple month's time.

It felt like *love*. It felt like a love stronger than I'd ever felt before. It felt so real, it's hard to imagine that it wasn't.

But here I am, staring at the clock and waiting for a man that I already know won't show up. Why would he? And after how he spoke to me last night, why would I want him to?

Am I that pathetic that I still want to see him, even though he accused me of setting him up and doing all of this for some stupid merger? *He's* the one who was so scared of getting fired from his daddy's little company that he came up with an elaborate plan to pretend to be *engaged* to me!

I shouldn't be upset about him.

I should be happy that I dodged a bullet. No, I didn't dodge a bullet. I dodged a fucking *rocket*.

I glance at the door one more time and then force myself to look away. I push my chair back, marching to Julia's office.

"Julia," I say as I poke my head in. "I think I'm going to take you up on that offer of the day off. I need to go home and be with my mom."

"Of course, Naomi," she says. "I'll cover your afternoon clients."

"I only have two appointments—my notes are on top of my desk."

She nods, and I slip out the door. I wave to Meg, who gives me a tight-lipped smile. I push the door open and fly down the stairs towards my car.

I know one thing: I need answers.

MID-MORNING TRAFFIC ISN'T BAD, so I make it home in decent time. When I race the steps up to my apartment, my heart is pounding. Running up a couple flights of stairs while you're panicking about your long-lost father and your failed fake engagement will do that to a person. Apparently.

"Mom?" I call out as I unlock the door.

"In here, honey," she says from the bedroom. I drop my bag and head towards her voice. The blinds are drawn. Her frail body hardly forms a lump under the covers and my breath catches in my throat.

The anger and frustration that was burning a hole in my chest dissipates, and I sit on the edge of the bed gently. My mother's eyes flutter open and she tries to smile at me.

"How's the nausea today?"

"Oh, it's not so bad," she lies. "I'm fine. Shouldn't you be at work?"

"I took the day off."

"Are you okay? You look like hell."

"Gee, thanks, Mom."

She chuckles, patting my hand. Her chuckle turns to a cough and she tries to sit up. I fluff her pillows and help her up.

"Have you eaten?"

"I had some toast this morning," she says. She gestures to the nightstand, and I see half a piece of toast. 'Some toast' meant half a slice with a bit of butter on it—hardly enough sustenance for a grown woman.

I nod. Suddenly, I'm tongue tied. I thought I would barge in here and demand answers, but what am I supposed to say?

My mother takes a deep breath, her eyes boring into me with a look that only mothers can give.

"Something happened between you and Max, didn't it?"

I snort bitterly. "How did you know?"

Tears well in my eyes and I shake my head.

"Who is my father, mom?"

"What?"

"I need to know. Who is he? How come you never told me?"

My mother sighs, staring towards the closed blinds and blinking back tears. She squeezes my fingers and then swings her head back towards me.

"I was scared, Naomi."

"Of what?"

"That you'd find him, and I'd have to see him again."

"What, why? What happened? Did he... did he do anything to you?" My voice is strangled. I'm so close to getting the answers I need. So close to finding out where I came from. So close to knowing why Max was so angry this morning.

My mom just sighs, squeezing my fingers again.

"No, no. Nothing like that." She looks at me and smiles sadly. "There's no chemotherapy for a broken heart, honey."

33

MAX

"WHAT DO YOU MEAN, you don't have a daughter? What about this?!"

I slam the folder on his desk, sitting back in my chair and waiting for his answer. He stares at me with dark eyes, and I search his face for any resemblance between him and his supposed daughter.

She has her mother's eyes, and her mother's lips. His nose, maybe?

He reaches forward and flips the folder open, glancing at it curiously. His eyebrows shoot up and then he looks at me.

"Private investigator?"

"It was my parents. They did it without my permission. But I'm glad they did, otherwise I never would have known what you two were up to."

His eyebrows stay raised and he glances back down at the folder.

"Naomi Rose," he muses. He reaches up and scratches the back of his head. My eyes widen—I've seen that movement before. Naomi does it anytime she's lost in thought.

My heart starts hammering and a lump forms in my throat.

It's true, then!

She lied to me. I'm simultaneously relieved and crushed. I can't speak.

Jerry flicks the first page over and his eyes widen.

"Jacqueline Rose?"

"Her mother."

"Her mother is Jacqueline Rose?" He inhales sharply, his whole body stiffening. He flicks through more pages, scanning the paperwork with almost panicked interest. Suddenly, I want it back. It seems so intrusive to have him reading all these things about Naomi.

Maybe this was a mistake.

"She's twenty-nine," he says to himself. "Oh my god..."

"What?"

"I just... I need to meet this woman. Where is Jackie? And Naomi? Holy shit." He stands up, grabbing his jacket.

Then he sits down, putting his hand to his forehead and staring at the center of his desk. He picks up the phone and then hangs it up again.

Finally, he swings his eyes over to me.

"How...? Oh my god."

"You... you didn't know?" Is he lying? Is this all part of the ruse? They must be playing me. She said she'd never met him, maybe they decided to pretend to have never met.

But his cheeks are red, and I can see a smattering of freckles across his nose. Maybe his grey hair used to be red? He puts his elbows on his desk and drops his head in his hands, shaking it slowly.

"Jackie," he whispers.

I watch him as my heart thumps, and I *know*.

I know that I was wrong.

Naomi was telling the truth.

They've never met.

There's no way someone could pretend to have that reaction. A tear drops from Jerry's eye and he brushes it away angrily. He looks at Naomi's picture from the folder, running his fingers over her face. Finally, as if he remembers that I'm there, he looks up and closes the folder, pushing it back towards me.

"Take me to her."

"What, now? I mean, we're not exactly speaking right now…"

"Take. Me. To. Her."

There's no question in his voice. I've heard that voice before, and I know that Jerry is just like my father—they're men who are used to getting what they want. I nod my chin and take the file back, sliding it into my jacket pocket.

"She's probably at work. You can ride with me if you want?" I watch his hands shake as he squeezes them into fists. He nods curtly, saying nothing.

I wonder if he still has a voice.

His assistant tries to call after him as we walk out, but he just waves over his head. "Cancel my appointments!" He yells out, and we walk into the elevator.

He doesn't look at me, and he doesn't speak. His face is pale and drawn, and his arms are crossed over his chest. We find my car and drive to Naomi's work in silence.

When I walk in, I see Meg right away. Her eyebrows shoot up and she rushes towards me. She stands in front of me, blocking the way. Her arms are crossed and she shakes her head.

"She's not here," she hisses. "You should go. How *dare* you!"

"Where is she?"

"I don't know, Max. Home, probably. Even if I knew, I wouldn't tell you. You should be ashamed of yourself. Get out."

I exchange a glance with Jerry.

I probably deserve that. The shame makes my cheeks burn.

How could I have been so wrong? I let my pride and my ego make me push away the only woman that's been decent to me. I chased her out of my house! I made her fucking cry!

My heart burns with guilt. We step back outside, and Jerry clears his throat.

"What was that about?"

"Naomi's a bit mad at me right now," I respond. That's probably the understatement of the century, but I'm not exactly feeling like sharing my deepest, darkest feelings with my new companion. We get back in my car and I head towards Naomi's apartment. If she isn't there, I'm not sure where she could be.

I know one thing: I need to find her. If not for me, then for Jerry. He deserves to meet his daughter, and she deserves to know who he is.

A sliver of hope enters my mind when I think of it. If I bring them together, maybe she'll forgive me for this morning. I shake my head and focus on the road. I can't let my mind run away from me.

"What's she like?" Jerry asks in the silence. I turn down the car radio and look at him. His cheeks have a bit more color, but he still looks nervous as hell.

I sigh. "She's incredible. Smart, funny, successful. She's gorgeous."

We're only a few minutes away from her house, and my heart is thumping. Jerry nods. "You love her?"

"Yeah," I reply, and we're quiet.

We don't speak until I pull up outside Naomi's apartment. I nod to the steps.

"Jackie's probably up there, too. She's been living at Naomi's since she started chemo."

"Chemo?" His eyes widen and his voice chokes. He glances at me and I see the panic in his face. "Chemo for what?"

"Breast cancer," I reply. "It was in the file."

"I missed that," he whispers. "I shouldn't be here. Fuck." He hangs on to the passenger's side door as if it's a life raft.

"Too late," I say. "We're here."

He glances at me and laughs bitterly. "I bet Jackie loves you," he says. "She always liked people with a bit of personality."

"I don't think she likes me very much right now."

Walking up the steps to her apartment building is like walking to both our funerals. Jerry's so pale, he looks like he's already died, and I can't think of anything except how I'm going to apologize to Naomi.

How can I apologize for that? I accused her of some ridiculous conspiracy and then I threw her out! I hesitate at the door, glancing at Jerry.

"You sure you want to do this?"

"Nope," he says, and then he presses the buzzer next to the name 'Rose'.

It only takes a minute for Naomi's voice to come through the intercom. Her voice sounds thin and distorted through the old audio equipment, but my heart still jumps.

"Yes?"

Jerry leans in. "Naomi, hi," he says. "You don't know me. I'm... I..." He glances at me. "My name is Jerry Irving."

He hesitates, and the intercom clicks. Did she hang up?

A second goes by, and then the buzzer sounds. I look at Jerry, who takes a deep breath and then pushes the door open.

34

NAOMI

My mother is patting her face, smoothing her clothes down and glancing around the room. We've moved to the living room to talk and she's got a blanket thrown over her legs.

"Hand me that scarf, quick," she says, pointing to a coat hanger. I do as she says and she wraps it around her head. "How does that look? Do I need some lipstick?"

"You look fine, Mom. What is he doing here? How did he find my apartment?"

"I don't know," she says, pinching her cheeks. She looks like she's hyperventilating.

I'm in shock. Ten minutes ago, she told me my father's name for the first time in my life. And now he's here? How did he even find my address?

None of this makes sense, but I don't have time to figure it out. A heavy hand knocks on the door. My mother yelps, and then takes a deep breath to compose herself. I wait until she nods to me, and then I open the door.

Jerry Irving is with Max. My eyes go from one to the other and my mouth opens and closes like a goldfish. Jerry—my father—is tall, with a thick head of grey hair. His eyes are dark brown, and he's got the look of a man who used to be in great shape in his youth.

His arms are stiff by his sides. He stares at me, wide-eyed.

"Naomi," he breathes.

"Hi." Do I call him Jerry? Calling him 'Dad' seems wrong. "You, uh, want to come in?"

He nods his head down, staring past me towards my mother. My eyes flick to Max, and I step aside to let the two men in. Jerry runs a hand through his hair, stepping inside and wiping his feet on the rug.

"Keep your shoes on, it's fine," I say. "You guys want some coffee?"

"Sure," Jerry says. "Thanks. I'm sorry to barge in like this." His gaze swings to my mom and I watch his eyes widen ever so slightly. "Hi, Jackie."

"Jerry," my mother says. Her earlier nervousness is completely gone. Her eyes are brighter than I've seen them in weeks. She lifts her hands towards Jerry, who practically runs towards her. He clasps her hands and sinks down on the sofa beside her.

"Jackie," he breathes. "You look fantastic."

My mother starts laughing and shakes her head. "You've always been a smooth talker. You don't have to lie. I know I look like I've been kicked in the ass by cancer."

"I'm not lying. How's... how's that going?"

"It's going."

My mother glances at me, and I slip into the kitchen to make some coffee. Her face is flushed, and she's still holding Jerry's hands. My heart is thumping. I don't know what to think. She told me that Jerry was the love of her life, and that he left to build his company. She wanted to live in the country and continue painting. They broke up right before she found out she was pregnant with me.

I put a filter in the machine and then get the feeling I'm being watched. I pause, turning my head to see Max in the doorway. I freeze, not trusting my hands or my voice.

I wish I had a monologue prepared for this moment. I wish I could tell him what I think of him, tell him what today was like for me.

But I've got nothing. I just turn back to the machine and pour some water into it and flick the machine on.

"I'm sorry, Naomi. I'm so sorry." His eyebrows are drawn together. I lean against the counter, folding my arms across my chest. He takes a deep breath. "I didn't know. It's not until I went to Jerry's office and spoke to him that I knew I was wrong. I'm so sorry."

I nod. "Thank you," I say. "I appreciate the apology." My voice sounds tense, even to my ears. Max runs his fingers through my hair and looks at me with those stupidly piercing blue eyes of his, and I hate how much I want to forgive him.

I turn to watch the coffee drip into the pot, not wanting to look at his annoyingly perfect face.

Finally, I take a deep breath.

"Why didn't you believe me?"

I glance over my shoulder. He crosses his arms, biting his thumbnail and staring at my old linoleum floors.

"I don't know."

"It hurt."

"I know."

The coffee machine gurgles, and I pour the steaming liquid into four mugs. I hand him two of them, grabbing the other two and nodding towards the living room. I'm not ready to forgive him. Just a few hours ago he was throwing me out like I was some lying scumbag. And now he comes here, to *my* house, with my *father* of all people! And he thinks I'm just going to fall over and forgive him?

I can't. I just can't. Not right now. Not like this.

I sit down across from my mom and Jerry, who both turn towards me. Max leans against the wall in my peripheral vision and I try to ignore the thumping of my heart. I'm being torn apart by so many different emotions right now, all I can do is sit down and breathe.

Jerry clears his throat.

"It's nice to meet you, Naomi."

I nod.

"I'm sorry... If I'd have known..."

"Mom told me that she kept me a secret from you," I interrupt. "I know you didn't know about me."

"I hope that maybe we can get to know each other?" His voice is hesitant. My mom has a hand on his thigh. She looks like she's still in love with him, even after all these years.

I nod. "Yeah, we can do that."

It comes out as a croak, and I clear my throat.

"Maybe I can take you out to lunch sometime. Maybe I can take you both out," he adds. My mother smiles. She squeezes his thigh.

"I think you and Naomi will have lots to talk about without me," she says gently.

As much as I want to ask him a million questions, I know it isn't the time. I force a smile and nod, and then get up.

"I'm going to give you guys some time to catch up. Max?" He jumps up, eyes wide. "I'll walk you to your car."

I slip into my room and grab the little black velvet box in my underwear drawer, and then follow Max out the front door.

Jerry and my mother are still staring at each other when we walk out. As soon as we leave the apartment, the tension between Max and I escalates. I fumble with my keys when we get to his car, staring at my hands and waiting to find the courage to say something.

"I'm sorry, Naomi," he whispers.

I finally meet his eye. I nod.

"I know. Thank you. And thanks for bringing my... Jerry around. Saved me looking him up."

We stare at each other for a few moments as Max's eyebrows draw together.

"I was hoping, maybe, we could hang out? I don't want this to be the end of us."

I smile sadly, shrugging. "What is 'us', Max? A pretend engagement? What are we going to do? Keep pretending? Or are we going to tell everyone the truth and then start dating from the beginning?" I shake my head. "Maybe this is a sign."

"A sign of what?"

"A sign that we should just let it go. I have a lot to deal with, with my mom and now, with Jerry. You've got your parents to deal with. Your new position at the company. This gives you an excuse to end the engagement without consequences. Let's just... leave it where it is."

"I don't want to leave it where it is, Naomi," he says, taking a step towards me. He reaches towards me but I take a step back. My throat starts to close and my heart feels like it's shattering more and more with every second that I stand out here. I shake my head slowly and watch the pain enter Max's eyes.

"Is this what you want?" He asks in a hoarse whisper.

I can't speak. I just nod, and pull the ring out of my pocket. When I hand him the box, his face crumples. He flicks the box open and stares at the ring, and then at me. His mouth opens, but he says nothing.

I turn away from him. I don't want him to see me cry. I

don't want to stay here with him, because then I might change my mind.

So I turn away, and I run back towards my apartment. As soon as I'm inside the building, I sit down on the staircase and let the tears flow. I watch him get into his car and drive away, and I cry some more.

I know it's better this way. It's simpler.

It's over.

35

MAX

It takes me three weeks to work up the courage to hand in my notice to my father. Quitting the family business is not something I thought I'd ever do, and by the look on my dad's face, he never thought I'd do it either.

But I have to do it.

Once Naomi left, what else was there to do? It's like she opened my eyes to what I was putting up with, to the mental games that my parents play. She made me realize how crazy this life really is. Why would I keep working for the company that tried to control my life like that?

I finally grow a pair. I'm a grown man, for Christ's sake. I can find a job on my own. If my parents cut me out of their will, then they cut me out. It's not worth living my entire life on a short leash just to get a payout.

Somewhere in the back of my mind, I know Naomi would be proud of me. She hasn't spoken to me since the day at her apartment, but the thought of her being happy for me gives me the courage to quit. Maybe I just tell myself that to make myself feel better, but it still helps me go through with the resignation.

My father's face is grim when I give him my notice. He takes the envelope from me, staring at it for a few minutes. He purses his lips and shakes his head.

"Is this because of the girl?"

"No. Well, maybe. I just need to be my own man, Dad. I thought you'd understand that."

He nods slowly. "There will always be a place for you here," he says as he shakes my hand. My chest feels tight, and a lump forms in my throat. I nod.

"Thanks, Dad."

"What are you going to do?"

I sigh. "I'm not sure yet. I want to pursue a career in football. If I'm not playing, I can still coach. I've got lots of contacts from college."

My dad extends his hand towards me. "I'm proud of you, son," he says. He tightens his grip on my hand and pulls me towards him, wrapping me in an unexpected hug. "You remind me of myself when I was your age."

"Just wait to see how I turn out before you say you're proud," I laugh. He grins at me, and the tightness in my chest eases.

A couple weeks later, when I walk out of the building on my last day, it's like a huge weight has been lifted off my shoulders. I know it was the right decision. And if I ever see Naomi again, I'll thank her for giving me the courage to do it.

"So I heard you're all finished up at daddy's company!" Graham asks as I walk into Joel's living room. It's Sunday, and me and the boys are all here to hang out and watch the games.

I fall onto the couch, grabbing the beer that Connor hands me. "Yep. Last day was Friday."

Joel whistles. "He's finally cutting the apron strings, boys," he laughs. "I'm happy for you, man."

"What are you going to do?" Graham asks. He tosses me a bag of chips and turns down the volume on the TV.

I shrug. "Been talking to my old college football coach. He said he might be able to get me on as an assistant coach for next season. Spring training starts in a couple months, so the timing would be good."

"Nice," Connor says, nodding. "Sounds like a good gig."

"Yeah, it will be. I walked into the athletics building at college last week to talk to him and it was like coming home. I spent so many hours in that building. It'll be nice to be around football again," I say. "I missed it."

"If your knee is better, you should join our rec team," Connor says. "You won't have that excuse anymore."

I grin. "It's not quite there yet, but maybe in the fall." I haven't found a physical therapist since Naomi, and progress on my knee has stalled. Even doing the exercises she showed me reminds me of her, and most days I avoid doing them.

None of my friends mention Naomi, which I'm grateful for. They haven't mentioned her since the weekend after it ended between her and I. The boys took me out for the weekend and got me completely wasted, and then helped to nurse my sorry, hungover self back to health with Gatorade and greasy breakfasts.

It seems like it all happened a lifetime ago, even though it's only been a few weeks. My heart was just as shattered as my knee. It's recovering slowly, but it's recovering.

EVENTUALLY, the rawness of the whole ordeal fades. My heart still skips a beat when I see a redhead in the street, or at the bar, or at the grocery store, but it doesn't hammer against my ribs quite so hard as it used to. I make it through the holidays without too many reminders of Naomi. My parents make a few comments that sting, but I try to ignore them.

I end up telling my dad that the private investigator was wrong about Naomi, and the acquisition of Jerry's company still goes through. I don't tell them my engagement was fake, only that we broke up because of the whole misunderstanding.

I don't know why I don't tell them the full truth. Maybe it seems wrong to reduce my time with Naomi to just a business arrangement. Even after everything, I don't want them to think that it was all fake.

Or maybe, it's *me* that doesn't want to think that. I want to believe that what we had was real. I want to believe that when she accidentally told me she loved me, it meant something.

I END up getting the job as an assistant coach at my old college, and come spring, we start the pre-season training in full force. By the beginning of March, I'm back on the grid-iron, running practices and feeling the familiar buzz of energy that comes with sports and competition.

Coach Carter pats me on the shoulder after one of the first practices, grinning.

"Good to have you back," he says.

I nod. "It feels good to be here. Thanks for taking a chance on me."

"You were a good player, and you'll be a good coach," he says. He looks me in the eye as a lump forms in my throat. We nod to each other, then he walks towards the locker rooms with the team.

I look around the stadium, up at the stands that will soon be full of fans, and I breathe in the crisp spring air. It feels good to be back. It feels good to be free of my parents, to be doing something for *me*. Who knows, maybe in a couple years I'll be a head coach. For the first time in a long time, the future is exciting.

I look up and down the field and let out a sigh before turning towards the locker rooms.

It's exciting to be here and it feels good to finally be my own man, but I know it would feel a lot better if I had someone to share it with. I pick up a water bottle that one of the players dropped, shaking my head to clear those thoughts.

I can't think like that. I have to keep moving forward.

36

NAOMI

"JACKIE and I were going through a rough patch," Jerry explains. "I wanted a career, and she wanted the opposite."

He sighs. I stab my fork into a piece of chicken, watching him.

"Her father pulled me aside one evening. I think he could tell that we were both unhappy. He gave me this long speech about relationships being about more than just love. He told me that our priorities needed to be in line, and that I wasn't doing anyone any favors by hanging around."

"Grandpa said that?"

Jerry nods, chuckling bitterly.

"Yeah. I broke up with your mother the week after that conversation. It was the hardest thing I ever did. I could tell that I broke her heart. I broke my own heart."

"And she never told you about me?"

He shakes his head, spinning his fork in his plate of pasta. A waiter glances at our table, and a couple at the table next to us bursts out laughing.

I feel like I'm in a bubble. It's like the world is going on around me and I'm not part of it, I'm just watching it happen. It's surreal being here, with Jerry, hearing these things.

"I never heard from Jackie after that. I moved to New York, and then down to Atlanta and over to Europe. I tried calling her, but she changed her number. Then, I guess I just stopped trying."

"That's understandable, I guess."

Jerry sighs.

"I think she was trying to protect you. Or maybe trying to protect herself. When I broke up with her, I betrayed her trust. I told her I didn't want a family, I just wanted a career."

"So that's why she never told you she was pregnant?"

"I guess so." His forehead creases, and his dark brown eyes fill with pain. He looks at me, taking a deep breath. "I wish she'd told me."

"Look, Jerry," I say. "Don't torture yourself about it. It was a long time ago, and by the sounds of it, you didn't have much choice."

"I could have tried harder to speak to her."

"Why would you? You thought you were broken up and that was that."

It's strange to be comforting my own father about the one thing that plagued me my whole life. His absence was like a splinter under my skin that I just couldn't get out. It just festered as the years went on, the pain of his leaving getting worse and worse. And now that he's here, I'm the one trying to make him feel better.

"I'm sorry, Naomi. I'm sorry I wasn't there. I missed so much."

I want to change the subject. I glance at his hand and note the absence of a ring.

"You never married?"

Jerry chuckles bitterly. "I was married three times."

"Oh."

"I always found some way to fuck it up—sorry. Screw it up."

"You can swear," I grin. "I'm a big girl."

He grins. "I don't know how to act right now. This is very weird for me."

"Don't worry, it's weird for me too."

His eyes lighten, and a smile breaks over his face. He chuckles, shaking his head. "You're a lot like her."

"Like my mom?"

"Mm," he nods. "She was the love of my life."

His words are like a spear through my heart. Jerry's eyes mist, and his hand trembles as he reaches for his glass of water. He takes a sip, dabbing his lips with his napkin and clearing his throat.

"Food is good," he says, nodding to his plate. "Good choice."

"Yeah," I say, looking around and trying to ignore the emotion choking my throat. "I found this place a couple years ago. My girlfriends and I come here for birthdays and stuff."

WHEN HE DROPS me off back home, my mother walks him back downstairs and I sink down on the couch.

That was hard.

Meeting him, spending time with him, hearing his side of the story—it's hard to take it all in. My entire life, it was one big question mark. And now, he seems so... *human*. He's not a monster, or a drug-addicted convict, or an abusive maniac. He's pretty normal.

A thin tendril of anger curls in my heart when I think about my mother. Why did she never tell him about me? Did she think she was protecting me?

I hear her labored footsteps coming up the stairs before the apartment door opens. Her eyes are shining and her cheeks are rosy. She hums to herself as she takes her shoes off, smiling at me as she brushes past towards the kitchen. I hear the kettle go on, and I take a deep breath.

She was protecting *herself*.

I think of Jerry's face when he told me she was the love of his life, and how my mom reacted when he first showed up at my apartment. I think of the spring in her step since he's been around, and how that compares with the darkness that clouded over her whenever I'd mention him when I was a kid.

Maybe *he* was the love of her life, too. And by cutting herself off completely, she thought she was protecting herself, and maybe me, from the pain of the heartbreak.

She denied me a relationship with my father, though. For decades.

I look over at her, and then sink down on the couch and close my eyes. I see Max's face in my mind's eye. He's combing his fingers through his hair, smiling that irresistible smile at me. My heart thumps as I imagine his voice, his smile, his touch.

A second later, my heart is breaking all over again. My mother clears her throat and I open my eyes to see her drop a cup of tea in front of me. I smile in thanks, and then I understand.

This is what she was protecting herself from. The heartbreak—the searing pain that cuts through my body every time I think of him. The feeling that the world is just a little bit duller, a little bit less colorful and less vibrant when he's not around.

Does it last forever?

I pick up the steaming mug of tea and take a sip. Mom sits

down in the recliner, staring out the window and smiling to herself. She has her hands clasped over her heart and a smile floating on her lips.

I think my mom was wrong to cut Jerry out of her life. For the millionth time, I wonder if I made a mistake with Max, too.

37

MAX

Before I know it, it's been three months since I quit my job and almost four months since I've seen Naomi.

"Westbrook!" Coach Carter says as I walk into the football wing of the athletic building. It still smells the way it did when I was a player—like sweat, cleaning supplies and dedication. Coach stands up and pokes his head out of his office. "Get in here, I want you to meet someone."

I drop my bag full of clipboards, game notes, athletic tape, and bits and pieces that I carry around with me for practice, and I follow him into his office.

As soon as I see that red hair pulled back in a high pony tail, I know it's her. I pause in the doorway. My stomach drops and my heart starts racing. I'm sure I look like a deer caught in the headlights, because Coach frowns. He waves me in impatiently.

"Come on, Westbrook. This is our new full-time physio company—PhysioFIT. Miss Rose here is the head physio over there. We were just developing a plan for the season. I was thinking you could be in charge of it."

He nods to me, waving me towards the chair. I gulp.

Naomi turns to see me and her eyes widen. She wipes her hands on her thighs and takes a deep breath before standing up.

"Max," she says. "Good to see you again."

"You two know each other?"

"I was Max's physical therapist for a while," she says quickly, smiling at Coach. "How's the knee?"

"It's going," I reply. I can't take my eyes off her. She's breathtaking. She's more beautiful than I remembered. I thought her face had been burned into my mind's eye forever, but my memory hadn't done her justice. She extends her hand, looking me square in the eye as she pumps my arm up and down.

"Good to see you again."

She sits back down, turning away from me and pointing back to a stack of papers. "We're proposing to have full-time junior physios on site for every game and every practice," she says to no one in particular. "I, or another senior physio will be here for the games as well."

"Excellent, excellent," Coach says. He glances at his watch and leans back in his chair to adjust his cargo pants down below his stomach. He's built like a tank, with the thick neck and meaty hands that betray a long career as a football player. He nods to Naomi. "I'll let you discuss the details with Westbrook here. I've got a few things to see to before practice. Glad to have you on board."

He extends his huge hand, engulfing Naomi's delicate one as they shake. She smiles at him and watches him walk out before finally lifting her pretty green eyes up to me.

"Hey," she says. "I wasn't expecting this."

"Neither was I."

"You... you're working here now?"

I clear my throat, nodding. "Quit my parents' company

right after..." I wave my hand between us. I can feel a blush creeping up my cheeks and I hate it. As usual, Naomi's got me feeling off-balance.

A smile twitches at the corners of her lips, and the edges of her eyes crinkle. She dips her chin down, looking up at me through her pretty, long lashes. "I'm happy for you. Spreading your wings."

"Finally flew the coop," I grin.

"Like a big boy," she laughs, and an arrow pierces my heart.

She takes a step towards me and my heart goes wild. When she puts her hand on my forearm, the touch sends my whole body reeling. She looks up at me, taking a deep breath. "I'm proud of you," she says. "The way your parents treated you wasn't right."

I nod. "How are things with your mom... and your dad?"

"They're good. Mom's in remission, and I've been keeping in contact with Jerry."

She looks like she's going to say something, but she closes her mouth and sighs. An awkward moment passes. I point my thumb over my shoulder.

"You want to grab a bite to eat? We can bring this paperwork and go over the work stuff, and then I can write it off as a business expense."

She laughs and my heart clenches again. "How could I resist?"

Warmth floods through me, and I nod my head out the door. "I need to be back in an hour for practice, but I know a little cafe nearby that has great sandwiches."

"Sounds perfect."

We fall into step beside each other. She holds her papers close to her chest and I wonder if it's to resist holding my hand. I feel her eyes on me and I glance over just in time to see her looking away.

As much as I've tried to convince myself that it was for the best to go our separate ways, I can't deny how good it feels to be next to her.

38

NAOMI

BY THE TIME our sandwiches arrive at the table, I've explained the entire business plan for the physical therapy partnership. Maybe I'm talking faster than usual because of the nerves, or maybe this coffee is just extra strong. My hands are shaking, though, so I keep them folded on the table.

"That all sounds good. Do these hours count as work experience for the physical therapy students that will be on board?"

"They do," I reply. "We already have over thirty applicants."

The waitress drops our sandwiches down in front of us and I smile at her. She walks away, and Max grins at me over the food.

"Can we stop talking about work now?"

"I thought this was a business lunch."

He chuckles. "It is." He takes a bite of his sandwich, nodding in appreciation. "So how's your mom?"

"She's really good. She just finished her chemo last month, and she's been recovering ever since. Still has checkups to go to, but the doctors are saying she's in remission."

"What does that mean, exactly?"

"It means she needs to keep making sure the cancer isn't growing, so she needs to be checked pretty often, but for now, she's good."

"Wow. And she's stronger?"

"Way stronger. I think having Jerry around has helped her, too," I grin. "Sounds like they had quite a passionate relationship."

"What happened?"

"He had a big-shot career and my mom was a struggling artist, so there was friction. Then, my mom got pregnant and she didn't want to hold him back. That's what she says, anyway. I think she was just scared that he would leave her, so she made the decision for him."

"Must run in the family."

I stop my sandwich midway to my mouth, glancing at Max.

"What's that supposed to mean?"

"Didn't you make that decision for us?"

"I didn't... That's different," I stutter.

His eyes are incredibly blue in this light. The intensity with which he's staring at me is making my head spin, but I can't look away. He reaches across the table and puts his strong hand over my wrist, stroking my skin tenderly.

"I meant what I said that morning, before it all went to shit," he says gently, squeezing my arm.

"What's that?"

"That I loved you."

I freeze. My heart races. *Loved, as in, past tense.*

I swallow. "You also meant what you said when you

thought I was part of some conspiracy to sabotage your parents' company."

He cringes, pulling his hand away. He stares out the window and lets out a big sigh.

Why do I do that? I lash out anytime someone gets too close. It's like I can sense that he wants to open up to me, so I just shut it down. I can see the pain in his face—I did that to him.

My whole body is itching to be near him. This lunch has been the sweetest torture, and I don't want it to end. Not like this.

"I'm sorry—" We both say it at the same time. My eyes widen just as he turns to look at me, and we both start laughing.

"I'm sorry, Max. I know that I pushed you away. It was just so crazy, and—"

"It's okay. I'm sorry too. I was an idiot to do that to you."

"Do what to me?"

"Make you go along with that whole engagement plan. It was destined to end in disaster. How could it not? I've gone over it so many times in my head and I just feel like an idiot."

I chuckle. I lift a finger and point it at him. "That's why I said we shouldn't have slept together. That was the kiss of death."

Max grins, and his eyes flash. "You didn't seem too upset about it when it was happening."

"I wasn't." A coil of heat curls in my stomach. I squeeze my thighs together under the table, picking up my sandwich and staring at it without taking a bite.

"Max," I start. I flick my eyes up to see him staring at me intently. He licks his lips, and the heat in my stomach blooms. I take a deep breath. "I meant it too. That morning."

If I wasn't staring at his face, I would miss the tiny twitch of his lip, and the microscopic widening of his eyes. Those tiny movements send my heart racing.

"Let's start over," he blurts.

"What?" I laugh. "Start what over?"

"This. Us. I miss having you around."

"You miss having me around?" I arch an eyebrow. "How romantic."

"I miss *you*," he says with a grin. "That any better?"

"Marginally."

Silence hangs between us. He slides his hand across the table, palm up. I stare at it for a second, and then slip my palm over his. He curls his fingers into mine and I close my eyes. His hand so deliciously warm, his touch so beautifully tender.

"Let me make you dinner." He squeezes my hand. His voice is soft and sexy. "We can have fancy wine that requires a corkscrew and everything."

That makes me laugh, and all the emotions that I've been trying to bottle up erupt inside me. My eyes start to mist, so I close them.

Suddenly, Max is beside me. His arms are around me and all I can smell is him. All I can feel is the heat of his body next to me, and all I can hear is the soft murmur of his voice.

Tears slide down my cheeks and I melt into him. His palm slides over my cheek, wiping my tears away. He stares at me for a moment, and the pieces of my broken heart start to fuse back together.

Then, he brings his face closer and I know it will heal. He presses his lips to mine and I wrap my arms around him, clinging onto him for dear life. His hand slides from my jaw to the nape of my neck, pulling me in for a deeper kiss.

The cafe melts away. The whole world disappears. I forget

who I am and where I'm sitting. All that matters is him, and me, and our kiss.

Our love.

He rests his forehead against mine, touching the tip of his nose against the tip of mine.

"I gotta go," he says. "Coach will kill me if I'm late, and then I'll never be able to expense this meal."

I laugh, pushing him away and shaking my head.

"Ever the romantic."

He's laughing as he picks up his jacket and our stack of notes. "That's me. Don't you miss being engaged to me?"

"Every day," I say. He turns to look at me as a smile spreads across his lips. He leans down and kisses me softly.

"Come on," he growls. "I'll walk you to your car. Dinner at my place tonight?"

A lump has mysteriously appeared in my throat, so all I can do is nod. He slips his hand into mine and I'm grateful for it, because tears have completely misted up my eyes. I'd probably walk into a pole if he wasn't there to guide me.

We kiss again when we get to my car. I watch him walk back towards the college athletics building, and then I smile.

I missed having him around, too.

39

MAX

When Naomi gets to my place, she's changed out of her work clothes and into casual jeans and a black tee-shirt. All the blood in my body rushes between my legs. She puts a hand on my shoulder and gets on her tip-toes to lay a gentle kiss on my cheek.

"So where's this fancy wine of yours?"

"Just here," I say. "I opened it to let it breathe."

"Of course you did."

She grins at me, kicking off her shoes and hooking her arm around my waist. I tuck her hair behind her ear, breathing in deeply as my heart does cartwheels in my chest.

"You smell like you," I breathe.

"Who else would I smell like?"

"You always have a retort, don't you?"

"You still sure you missed me?"

I chuckle, dropping my hands to her waist and pulling her closer. "Yeah," I say. "I'm sure."

Creases appear on her porcelain forehead. Her eyebrows draw together and she tilts her chin up to study my face. She takes a deep breath. I feel her chest move against mine. She still has her arms hooked around my waist, and I feel her fingers curl into my shirt.

"What are we doing, Max? What is this?"

I drop my hand, finding hers and guiding her towards the couch. I've already laid out the wine and two glasses, so we both sit down. I pour us two glasses and hand her one, and then I look her in the eyes.

As many times as I practiced saying this over the months, and as sure of myself as I was an hour ago, right now is different. With her bright eyes staring at me, my certainty evaporates and my whole body starts to stress. My palms are sweaty, and I brush my hair back with my fingers.

"Naomi," I start. I need to stop and take a breath. She puts her glass of wine down and places her hands on my thighs. Her touch helps, and I can keep talking. "I fucked up. I know I did. Before, with you, I didn't act right. I shouldn't have put you in that position and I shouldn't have accused you of those things. I was a coward with anything relating to my parents."

"Max..."

I shake my head. "It's true. It wasn't until you left that I realized how special you are. You gave me the courage to quit working for my father, and to pursue what I really want. You showed me what matters. You," I say, tucking my finger under her chin. "Are incredible."

"I also fixed your knee, if we're listing my accomplishments."

I chuckle, and my nerves evaporate. She takes my glass of wine from my hands and puts it beside hers on the table, and then slides her hands into mine.

"Let's just start over," she says. "Just like you said."

"You and me. We can date. No engagement, no pressure, no contract. Just you and me."

"Just you and me."

A smile spreads across her face and her eyes twinkle.

"Is this a terrible idea?" She asks. "I can't tell. It feels like a great idea, but I've been wrong about these things before, especially with you. You've got a way of making me forget about common sense."

"Funny," I reply. "You have the same effect on me."

She laughs until I stop her with a kiss. She wraps her arms around my neck. I lean forward until she's laying down on the couch and I lean on top of her. I drop my arm to her waist and roll my hips towards her. Her body feels just as good as I remembered.

No, it feels better.

She deepens her kiss, tangling her fingers into my hair. Her back arches and her breasts press against my chest.

I knew this would happen when she agreed to have dinner at my place. Well, I hoped it would happen. But now that she's here in my arms? My body is going wild.

My heart is thumping, and my cock is rock fucking hard. Every time her fingers brush against an inch of skin, they set it on fire. I can't get enough of her. I kiss her harder and she moans into my mouth.

Her hips press against me and I feel the heat radiating between her legs. She spreads her legs and squeezes them around me, sending another wave of heat through my body.

"Max," she pants.

"Yeah, baby?"

"I missed you."

"I missed you too."

"And I missed your cock."

I grin. "My cock missed you too."

She laughs as I drop my hand between her legs. I wish we weren't wearing so many clothes. My fingers run along the inside of her thigh as she closes her eyes and drops her mouth open. She lets out a soft sigh as I reach the apex of her thighs and lay my palm between her legs.

I want to savor every minute of this. I want to etch every touch, every sound, every smell into my brain so I never forget it. I want to worship her body and make her feel like a fucking queen.

I want to hold her, and never let her go.

I tear her jeans off, running my fingers up her silky thighs until I reach her sopping wet panties. They're clinging to her lips as she shivers underneath me. I push her panties aside and feel the velvety wetness of her slit. She moans when my skin touches hers, rolling her hips towards me. She shivers when I roll her bud under my thumb, opening her eyes and panting. The emerald green of her irises looks almost hazy as she runs her fingers through my hair.

I drop my head between her breasts, inhaling her scent as she pushes back against my hand. When I slip my fingers inside her, she gasps.

This is heaven. It has to be. How else could I explain it? Watching the woman I love get closer and closer to orgasm— I love her. I know that. I've always known it, even when I tried to convince myself otherwise. Her back arches, and her walls clamp down around my fingers with surprising strength. Her honey covers my hand as she presses herself into me, digging her fingers into my shoulders. My lips find hers and she kisses me fervently.

I twirl my fingers around her bud, loving the way she moans at my touch. I kiss her again until her mouth falls open and I feel the orgasm wash over her.

I smile as my cock throbs. Fuck, she's gorgeous.

When she opens her eyes again, she stares at me and grins.

"My turn."

40

NAOMI

I'VE MISSED THIS—OUR sex. I've missed it all. Lazy mornings with him, long evenings talking, or even the times where we said nothing at all.

But the sex... the sex I've definitely missed. I've tried to pretend that I wasn't missing it, but my body has felt like a shell of what it was when we were together.

Within minutes, he's ignited the fire inside me again.

I can feel his length against my stomach, and all I want to do is make him feel as good as he makes me feel. Whatever is between us, as confusing as it is, I know it's real. It's *love*.

We wouldn't be here if it wasn't.

It only takes a couple frenzied seconds for us to get all our clothes off. My hands are around his shaft in an instant. He groans when he sees me moving closer to it. When I take it in my mouth, he sighs, running his hand across my shoulder.

"That feels so good, Naomi," he moans.

I make a noise in response, wrapping my fingers around the base of his shaft. I love making him feel good. I like seeing this big, powerful man melt at my touch. It turns me on so much to know that I'm doing this to him—these noises and moans and sighs that he's making—that's because of *me*.

He lifts my head off him, shaking his own.

"You're not getting away without me being inside you," he growls.

I grin. "Wouldn't dream of it."

He picks me up easily and I wrap my legs around his waist. He carries me to the bedroom and lays me down, groaning as he leans his body over mine.

"You have no idea how many times I've dreamt of this."

"I have some idea," I respond.

"Yeah?"

"Yeah. Probably half as many times as I have."

He chuckles, brushing his lips against mine. He shifts his body and I feel the tip of his cock brush against my slit. I shiver, spreading my legs and wrapping them around his waist. The feeling of his skin against mine is intoxicating.

When he enters me, the whole world disappears. I sigh in contentment, melting into the pillows and wrapping my body around his. We move as one.

When I come, I know that Max is the man for me. I know that there's nowhere else I want to be other than his arms. I know that there is no one else, nowhere else, nothing else that will make me feel as good as being right here in his arms.

The pleasure heightens my emotion—or maybe it's the other way around. Maybe it's knowing that I don't have to fight it, I can be with him. I can let myself love him fully and completely.

Once I let myself do that, my orgasm floods through me like a dam breaking. It crashes into me without hesitation, carrying me into a world of ecstasy. My body holds onto his and he moans into my skin. His teeth drag across my shoulder, and I feel him get harder as he drives himself deeper into me.

We're panting, sticky with the sweat and heat of our desire. Of our pleasure.

Of our love.

When it's over, he stays inside me and kisses me tenderly. He slides off me, draping his arm across my chest and sighing as his head hits the pillow.

"I think I needed that," he groans.

"I *definitely* needed that," I laugh. "Haven't had an orgasm in way too long."

"No?"

I snort. "Well, I haven't exactly dated anyone since you," I admit. "And I guess I just didn't really feel like masturbating unless entirely necessary."

His fingers caress my collar bone, and I turn to look at him. I smile.

"I haven't been with anyone either," he admits. "I couldn't even look at other women after you."

"So I guess we're stuck with each other, then," I grin.

"I guess so. You wanna save some time and get married?" His eyes flash and a grin spreads across his lips.

I laugh, pushing his shoulder and swinging my legs over the edge of the bed. "No. Not yet. Not for a while."

"I can deal with 'not yet'," he grins.

"You think that wine has breathed enough?"

"I'd say so," he grins.

"I'll go get cleaned up and grab our glasses," I say. He smiles at me, and I slip into a towel. I go to the bathroom to wash our sex off my body, and then tip toe to the living room to grab the wine. I can see some food he's laid out on the counter and I go to investigate.

I smile when I see bruschetta. I stuff one piece in my mouth and carry the platter over with one glass of wine. I set the glass on his side of the bed, jogging back out to grab my own.

"Dinner in bed," I grin as I come back in. He's already chewing on a piece of bruschetta, nodding at me and wiggling his eyebrows.

"Starving," he says with his mouth full.

"Me too," I say, grabbing another piece.

"I've got some salmon for us, should only take a few minutes to cook up."

"Let's just eat this, and drink these," I say, lifting my glass. "And then we can reassess."

He arches his eyebrow, and I grin.

"You never know what we might want to do after a little snack."

"I've got a couple ideas," he says, lifting my hand and pressing his lips against my fingers. His hand drifts up my arm, sending a shiver of desire through me.

I smile, sip my wine, and let the happiness permeate my entire body.

In the darkest corners of my mind, I'd hoped this would happen. I wanted to come back to him. I wanted to leave our past behind us and start fresh, but I didn't believe it could happen.

Watching Max crunch on another piece of bruschetta makes me realize that it is possible to start over. Not only it is possible, it's happening.

He smiles at me again, and clinks his glass against mine.

"To us," he says.

"To us."

We drink our wine, and eat our food, and then I lean into

the man I love and wrap my arms around him. He pulls me on top of him and we forget about dinner for a little while. We've got more important things to take care of.

EPILOGUE
MAX

When I invite Naomi over to my parents' house, I see my mother's eyebrows raise ever so slightly in surprise. To their credit, my parents don't make any untoward comments. I think they were disappointed when it didn't work out between us, and they're happy to see us together.

Ever since I quit the company, they've given me a lot more space. It feels good to have my own job, and to be my own man. I think my parents, for all their faults, understand that. I think they respect it, too.

Naomi's mom is happy, too. She doesn't hide it as well as my parents. She wraps her arms around me and lays a big, sloppy kiss on my cheek whenever she sees me. Her eyes are brighter than they were when we first met, and when I see her with Jerry, I understand why. They look as starry-eyed as I feel when I look at Naomi.

Naomi moves in with me, and her mother spends a lot of time at her apartment. She says it's for doctor's appointments, but I think it might have something to do with Jerry.

The partnership between PhysioFIT and my football team works perfectly, and we renew the contract for another year. I tell Coach Carter about Naomi and me right away, and he just grins at me.

Life just slips into place. It feels natural.

ONE SUNNY SUMMER morning a few months after we decide to start over, Naomi wakes me up by wrapping her arms around me.

"I have a surprise for you," she says.

I open my eyes one at a time, clearing the sleep from my throat. She's grinning like the Cheshire Cat, and I look at her suspiciously.

"I thought you hated surprises."

"I hate being on the receiving end of surprises," she says. "I like giving them."

I grin, wrapping my arms around her and pulling her down beside me. She yelps, laughing as I roll on top of her.

"Five more minutes," I groan, closing my eyes and clamping my arms around her.

"Come on," she laughs, poking me in the side. "Get up, get up, get up!"

I groan, trying to stop the smile from spreading on my face. "Fine. What's this surprise?"

Naomi grabs my hand and pulls me out of bed. She smiles at me, nodding towards the living room. When I walk out, I notice the couch has been moved and she's cleared a space in the corner. There's a yoga mat on the ground, and a foam roller with a few bands hanging off the wall.

"Your very own physio corner!" She proclaims. "I bought all the stuff online and set it up this morning. You've been slacking on your knee."

"I thought this surprise would be nice and romantic," I say, rubbing my eyes. "This just looks like work."

Naomi wraps her arms around my waist and lays a soft kiss on my lips. "It is work, but I remember you saying that Connor had asked you to be on his fall football team. The season starts in three months, and I think we can get your knee strong enough to play."

My heart jumps. "Yeah?"

She nods. "I can work with you right here at home. I've developed a plan that I think should get you well enough to play by September."

My eyes widen as I look at the little physical therapy corner she's made. I tighten my arm around her as my throat closes with emotion.

"Naomi..."

She smiles. "Come on, let me show you. So I bought a foam roller and one of these spiky balls that you hate."

"Great," I say. Naomi laughs. She explains what all the things are for, and walks me through her plan for the next few months. I sit down and rub my hand over my knee, watching her stretch one of the rubber bands and demonstrate a new exercise for me.

My heart grows in my chest as I watch her.

She's incredible. Thoughtful, smart, dedicated, and all mine. I feel like I've won the lottery. When she's finished her demonstration, she stands up and puts her hands on her hips, looking at the equipment and smiling at me.

"So what do you think?"

I stand up and wrap my arms around her. "I think you're the best thing that ever happened to me."

She smiles and tilts her chin up. I kiss her, holding her close to me and feeling my heart beat along with hers.

IT TAKES ALMOST three years for me to propose to her again.

My heart thumps when I open the little black velvet box and show her my grandmother's ring once again. I'm down on one knee, proposing to her how I should have done it the first time.

"Get up, you goon," she laughs with tears in her eyes. "Of course I'll marry you. But I'm not signing any stupid contracts this time."

"Good. I wouldn't want you to."

I slip the ring on her finger. This time, she doesn't look scared. She doesn't look overwhelmed. She looks as happy as I feel.

I kiss the woman of my dreams for the millionth time. And for the millionth time, my whole body thrums for her, and my heart beats faster. This time, I'm not going to lose her.

This time, I'm going to marry the love of my life.

Thank you for reading! Keep reading for a preview of Book 2 of the Mr. Right Series: Engaged to Mr. Wrong

Get extended epilogues and deleted scenes from all my books by signing up for my newsletter. You'll , regular updates and new release alerts. Just type this URL into your browser:
http://eepurl.com/ddxnWL

xox Lilian
www.lilianmonroe.com
Facebook: @MonroeRomance
Instagram: @lilian.monroe

ENGAGED to

A Sports Romance

Mr. Wrong

Mr. Right Series: Book 2

LILIAN MONROE

ENGAGED TO MR. WRONG

A FAKE MARRIAGE ROMANCE

LILIAN MONROE

DESCRIPTION

I'm marrying the wrong man.
And the worst part?
I don't realise it until I meet his brother.

Both Elijah and Jesse are NFL quarterbacks, and their animosity runs deeper than sibling rivalry.
When my engagement to Elijah falls apart, I find myself caught in the middle of their bad blood.

I should just walk away.
This is beyond scandalous.
It shouldn't matter that Jessy cares about what I think, and he respects what I do.
It shouldn't matter that he makes my body thrum with need.
It shouldn't matter that he's turning on a part of me that I never knew existed.

I should really, *really* just leave it all behind.

And I do. I pack my bags and I walk away. It's over.

... Until I walk straight into Jesse's arms, and my whole world turns upside down.

Engaged to Mr. Wrong is a sizzling-hot sports romance. If you like billionaire bad boys with hearts of gold, you'll love this page turner. Grab Book 2 of the Mr. Right Series!

1. FARRAH

MY BIG DIAMOND ring sparkles in the dim sunlight as I grip my thigh. Elijah revs the engine and speeds up on the snowy, winding road up to his parents' cabin. I tighten my grip, one hand on my thigh and the other on the car's door handle. I close my eyes for an instant as my stomach lurches up to my throat.

Mr. Moose, my French bulldog, whines in the backseat as the car speeds around another bend. I glance back at him and my heart squeezes. He's shaking, and he looks as terrified as I feel.

"Babe, do you think you could slow down a little? We're not in any rush." My voice sounds weak and timid, even to my ears. Trees whip past us in a blur as he angles around another curve. "Moose is scared."

Instead of answering, he drops his foot down and the car throws me back further into my seat. I take a deep breath, tears gathering in the corners of my eyes.

I hate the way he drives.

I'm not sure if he accelerated on purpose, but it still hurts to be ignored. I cling to the side of the door and take deep breaths as the car swings me from one side to the other.

"Elijah—"

"I know what I'm doing."

"I know, babe, it's just..."

"What?" We make another turn and I'm flung the other way. I take a deep breath, trying to calm the hammering of my heart. I open one eye, glancing out the window at the sheer cliff face to our right. One split second decision could send us hurling down that valley.

I can't think like that.

"I would just really prefer it if we slowed down. I want to enjoy the view."

Elijah's face hardens as his lips form a thin line. His hands tighten on the steering wheel until his knuckles turn white. The tension ripples through his forearms as he keeps up the breakneck speed through the forest road.

"It was your decision to bring Moose. If we'd have left him at the kennel like I said, he wouldn't be scared right now."

But I would be.

I take a deep breath, blinking away the tears. Music is blaring on the radio, and it only makes my heart rate speed up.

We make another turn, and a big eighteen-wheeler truck appears in front of us. I know Elijah will want to overtake the truck, even on a snowy, winding forest road. I close my eyes and grit my teeth. I can feel the car inching towards the left, and Elijah leans his body over to look past the truck.

We're going to overtake it. I know we are. It's a double yellow line, with low visibility and a dangerous road, but I can feel Elijah's movements beside me.

I can't say anything. Look what happened last time I spoke up! He stepped on the gas and sped up. We get closer to the truck and I steal a glance over at my fiancé. His eyes are glued on the road. We inch over the center line and I close my eyes.

He presses on the accelerator and I make a silent prayer.

I don't want to die.

Not like this.

Not out of control, speeding down a road in dangerous conditions. Not with my dog terrified in the backseat. I grind my teeth together until I feel the car lurch back towards the right, breathing heavily.

Elijah lets out a loud *whoop* and then looks over at me. He's grinning from ear to ear.

"What do you think about that?"

I just grimace in response. I can't manage a smile right now.

BY THE TIME we get to his parents' cabin in upstate New York, I feel like I want to kiss the ground. I stumble out of the car and stretch my neck, keeping my back to Elijah as I wipe the last tears from my eyes. I turn to the back door of the car and open it up. Mr. Moose leaps into my arms and I rub his head. He's shaking like a leaf, and the anger in my stomach swells.

The front doors fling open and Elijah's mother walks out with wide open arms.

I'll talk to him about the driving tonight when we're alone. For now, I need to put on my best 'with the in-laws' personality.

So, I just plaster a smile on my face and turn to Mrs. Matthews. She's beaming.

"Elijah! Honey! And Farrah! Come in, come in," she says, waving us forward. "Don't worry about the bags, Gerard will get those for us. Gerard!" She turns around and calls out into the hallway. An older gentleman in a crisp suit appears.

He nods to Mrs. Matthews and heads towards the car.

I take a deep breath as Elijah comes around the car towards me. He snakes his arm around my back and kisses my temple.

"You didn't tell me you guys had a butler," I whisper to him.

"He's a concierge. Come on, let's go inside."

I nod, forcing a smile on my face. I clench my fists to stop my hands from shaking, drawing comfort from my dog's warmth. He's not trembling so hard anymore. Elijah rubs my lower back and kisses my temple again.

How can he be so tender now after being so inconsiderate in the car? Is it just because his mother is here?

I shake off the thought and follow him towards the cabin.

Well, *cabin* is probably the wrong word for it. More like forest-themed mansion. The massive building is made of huge logs stacked on top of each other. It's perched on a hill, surrounded by lush pine forests on three sides. There are huge bay windows reaching up to an A-line roof, and I can see the same windows all the way through the great room on the other side. The view of Lake Ontario through the house looks incredible.

The 'cabin' is about three times bigger than our place in Hoboken, New Jersey, which is saying a lot. Well—bigger than Elijah's place. He's the one on the NFL quarterback's salary and the big mansion and gleaming cars.

I'm a financial manager for a big construction company, so I do alright for myself. Realistically, though, Elijah's salary could support us both many times over.

Mrs. Matthews is waiting for us in the foyer. I put Moose down as he goes to greet Elijah's mother. He sniffs her curiously as she scratches his ear, and I breathe a sigh of relief. At least she seems to like dogs more than Elijah does. We kick off our boots and shed our layers of winter clothes before Mrs. Matthews wraps us both in big hugs.

I'm always surprised by the strength of her embrace. For such a slender woman, she's very strong. She waves us forward, all the while babbling about the weather and the drive and the problems they've had with the gas supply.

"The drive was fine," Elijah said. "Made it here in just under three hours."

"Under three hours!" Mrs. Matthews says, turning around and looking at us, wide-eyed. "Goodness, that's fast."

"Yes," I agree, stealing a glance at Elijah. He ignores me.

We make our way down a short hallway until we get to the huge, L-shaped kitchen, living, and dining area. The roof is at least three stories high, with huge exposed beams and rafters that give the whole place a chic, rustic feel. It seems wrong to describe this palace as 'rustic', but I can tell that's the look they're going for.

Mrs. Matthews hands me a mug of mulled wine with a smile. I wrap my fingers around the warm mug and inhale deeply.

"Smells incredible," I say with a smile. She must have forgotten that I don't drink, but I don't want to be rude. "Did you make it yourself, Mrs. Matthews?"

She just laughs, and then nods to the grey-haired woman who enters through a swinging door. "Maria made it all," Mrs. Matthews says. "She's an angel. And please, for the last time, call me Shannon!"

"Sorry," I smile. "Shannon."

Maria places a huge tray down on the carved wood dining table. She's in her sixties, I think, and has a no-nonsense look about her. She looks at me straight in the eye and then gives me a once-over with laser-sharp eyes. I stand a bit straighter. Then, she nods to the tray of food. It's laden with hot appetizers and dips and an assortment of veggies. She nods to us and ducks back through the swinging doors.

I feel like I've entered an alternate universe. This is so different from Christmas at my family's place that it doesn't even feel like the same world.

The thought almost makes me laugh. Here, no one is belligerent, no one is crying. There isn't the smell of whiskey on anyone's breath. It's... pleasant.

My belly rumbles and I walk over to Maria's food. I choose a carrot stick and a mini quiche, and sit down beside Elijah on the couch. I listen as he and his mother talk about everything and nothing. My gaze drifts out towards the windows. They're frosted at the edges, giving the impression of a wintry frame. It makes the dark, stormy water look even colder than it already does.

I shiver involuntarily, bringing my mug of mulled wine up to my nose to warm me up.

"So where's Dad?" Elijah asks, throwing a mini spring roll in his mouth.

"Oh, he and Jesse are out chopping some wood for the fire. They should be back any minute."

"Should Dad be chopping wood? Couldn't that throw out his back again?"

Shannon waves a hand, sitting down across from us and smoothing her pants down over her thighs. "You know how your father is. And speak of the devil! Here's Bruce!" She exclaims as the French doors open. A cold draft of air blows into the living room as Elijah's father appears.

He's wrapped up from head to toe in thick, wooly clothing. Only his eyes are visible, and he's leaning on a black cane. I can spot a wagon-full of freshly-chopped wood behind him. He rests the cane against the wall and turns towards us.

"Brr!" He says, looking over at us and pulling his wool scarf down. "Chilly out there!"

"Storm's coming," Shannon agrees. Bruce pulls the little wagon of wood through the door. Elijah and I jump up to help stack it near the living room fireplace.

"Where's Jesse?" Elijah asks, hauling half a dozen logs across the room. I grab two and follow his footsteps towards the huge stone fireplace.

"He went for a shower to wash up after all the chopping. He did most of it," Bruce laughs. "I'm not the man I used to be."

He kicks off his boots and helps us with the firewood. I follow Elijah towards the other end of the room, holding my small load of logs. Once he's stacked his, he turns towards me and grabs the wood out of my arms.

I yelp as a sharp, needling pain goes through my palm. Elijah must have pulled the wood away a bit too forcefully, because a splinter of wood buries itself into my hand. I pull my palm away, inhaling sharply and cradling my hand. Moose lets out a small bark and comes trotting up towards me, placing his front paws on my legs and staring up at me.

"What's wrong?" Elijah says, frowning at me. He stacks the logs neatly next to the hearth and turns towards me, placing his hands on his hips.

I grit my teeth, opening my palm towards him. It hurts to stretch my fingers. A huge, inch-long splinter is visible under my skin.

"Splinter."

Elijah frowns. Bruce appears next to me and starts stacking his logs. "What's going on?"

"I got a bit of a splinter," I explain. "Have you guys got tweezers?"

"Oh you poor dear," Shannon exclaims, appearing beside me. They all crowd around my hand. "We have a first aid kit in the pool house out back, otherwise I can run upstairs and get my tweezers."

Elijah brushes past me to get some more firewood from the stack near the French doors. I watch him walk away from me and my chest stings.

I know my splinter is just a minor injury and his mother is taking care of me. Still, watching my fiancé walk away as if he doesn't care hurts more than the shard of wood in my palm.

I force a smile. "Where's the pool house? I can just run out and get the first aid kit."

"Oh, I'll help you," Shannon says, leading me back towards the French doors. "Put these boots on, they'll fit you," she says, shoving furry boots towards me.

Maria appears in the doorway. "Mrs. Matthews," she says. "You're needed in the kitchen."

Shannon turns towards me and I smile. "Go ahead," I say. "Is that the pool house over there?" I point to the big building in the backyard.

"That's the one. The first aid kit is just under the sink in the kitchen."

"Thanks."

Elijah is beside me, loading up his arms with firewood. He glances at me and nods, then walks back towards the fireplace.

Guess he's not going to help me. I brace myself against the cold and open the doors, and then sprint towards the building across the lawn.

2. JESSE

I KNEW that I'd be chopping most of the wood, with Dad's bad back and all, but I hadn't anticipated how sweaty I'd get. Thank fuck for hot showers. As soon as I stopped moving, the sweat had frozen against my skin. The steamy hot shower is just what I need to thaw out my frigid body. Once I'm clean and warm, I turn the shower head off and open the curtain, brushing my thick mop of hair back off my forehead.

"Ah, fuck," I say under my breath. I forgot a towel. I'll have to walk out into the cold living room and over to the linen closet now, freezing my ass off all over again in the process. So much for the warming effects of the shower.

When I open the bathroom door, the steam billows out in thick white swirls. The cold hits my damp skin and sends shivers straight through me. I jog down the hall towards the linen closet, exhaling loudly as I try to ignore the freezing cold air.

I swing the linen door open and bend down to find a towel.

That's when I hear it.

Rustling.

Rummaging.

Movement.

Someone is here.

I grab the first towel I see and wrap it around my waist. Then, I lean back and peer around the open closet door. My eyes widen when I see the most beautiful woman I've ever seen standing near the kitchen sink.

Who. Is. That.

She's got long brown hair—it's almost black. It frames her face and gives her an ethereal look. Her dark, almond-shaped eyes are wide as she stares directly at me.

"I didn't see anything," she stammers, and I know that she did, in fact, see something. A blush stains her cheeks as her eyes drop down to my chest, and then she looks away.

"I'm just here for the first aid kit."

"Is someone injured?"

"Yes. I mean, no." She looks at the floor, and then the couch, and finally turns towards the sink. "I got a splinter."

Who is she? What is she doing here? One of my mother's friends, perhaps? She seems too young for that. A friend's daughter? I take a few steps towards her and let my eyes drift down her perfect figure. She's wearing a thin sweater and skin-tight jeans, and *damn*, she looks good. I walk towards her and she pointedly avoids looking in my direction.

"A splinter?"

She glances at me, then at my chest, then at my towel, and finally takes a deep breath. She nods.

"Well why'd you go and do that?"

Her eyes glimmer. "I could almost say it's *your* fault. You chopped the wood, did you not?"

"I did," I grin. I lean against the counter as I watch her fumble with the latches on the first aid kit. She inhales sharply, pulling her hand away and looking at her palm. I take another step towards her and take her hand gently in mine.

"Here," I say. "Let me help."

I ignore the ripple of electricity that passes through my arm when my skin touches hers. Did she feel it too?

She bites her lip and my cock throbs. She is *hot*. Her hand is small and delicate, and my palms feel rough against her soft skin. She's staring at me with those big, dark eyes of hers, and I'm loving the way they keep drifting down to my body. I see her gaze drop to my arms and I automatically flex my muscles.

She takes a deep breath and pulls her hand away.

"It's nothing." She shakes her head.

"It's about an inch long," I say. "It must hurt like a motherfucker."

She laughs, then, and her whole face lights up. She bites her lip, as if she's embarrassed to be laughing, and finally nods.

"It does hurt like a motherfucker," she laughs. "You're right."

Hearing such a pretty woman say something like that sends a thrill through my body. I wonder what she'd sound like if she were saying dirty, dirty things in my ear.

I shake my head, turning towards the first aid kit. I flip it open and find the tweezers.

"You can... shouldn't you get dressed? You're still wet. Aren't you cold?"

I look down at my body. It's covered in goosebumps, and I realize that yes, I am cold. But I don't want to let this woman out of my sight for a second, so I just shrug.

"I'm fine." I find the tweezers and hold out my hand. When she places her hand in my palm, another thrill passes through me. She's staring at my chest again, and she's blushing. Why is that turning me on so much?

I shake my head and turn to her splinter. "Here, come closer," I say, flicking on a light switch above the stove. She takes a step towards me, and I can smell the sweet perfume she's wearing. My whole body feels like it's pulled taut.

I bring her palm closer to the light, ignoring the heat that's pooling at the base of my spine. My cock is rock hard, and suddenly I wish I was wearing more than just a towel. She makes a noise when I nudge the end of the splinter.

"Sorry," I say, glancing up at her.

She shakes her head. "It's fine. I'm a wuss."

"You're not a wuss," I chuckle. "This thing would have me in tears. You ready?"

"Get that fucker out of me," she grins. "Come on. Do it."

God, that's hot. I grin, loving the way her eyes are sparkling. She takes a deep breath and squeezes her eyes shut, and I turn to her palm. I grab the end of the splinter with the tweezers and pull it out in one smooth motion. She groans as it comes out, and then exhales. She pulls her hand away to cradle it against her chest. Her eyes are watering and she's shaking her head.

"That was sore."

"Sorry."

"It's not your fault."

"That's not what you said when you first walked in."

She grins. "Well, you've redeemed yourself. Thank you for helping me."

Her eyes linger on mine, and then on my lips. Her cheeks flush again, and I try to ignore the steel rod between my legs. I clear my throat.

"Here," I say, pulling out some alcohol and gauze. "We should clean it."

Neither of us says anything as I clean the small wound. She inhales sharply as the alcohol touches her skin, leaning towards me. I run the cotton ball softly over her injury as I cradle her palm in mine. Then, I take some gauze and tape and I cover the splinter wound.

"There," I say, keeping her hand in mine. "All better."

She's blushing again, and I'm trying to ignore the throbbing between my legs. She smiles. We stare at each other for a few moments. I'm still holding her hand, and I don't want to let it go.

"You want me to kiss it better?"

"You asking for a slap across the face?" She laughs.

Her eyes flick down to my lips and a sizzle of heat runs down my spine.

She points to my chest. "What happened here?" Her fingers just brush against my damp skin before she pulls them away. She drops her other hand from mine. "Sorry."

"It's fine," I say, wishing she was still touching me. Her fingers ran the length of the long, jagged scar that cuts across the left side of my chest from collarbone to sternum. "Happened when I was a kid. My brother and I were horsing around. It was an accident." *Or at least that's what I always say.* Her eyes widen and her mouth drops, as if she's remembering something.

She shakes her head.

"I'm sorry, I never introduced myself. You're Jesse, right? I'm Farrah. I'm Elijah's girlfr—fiancée."

Oh. Fuck.

"Ah, of course! I thought you were a bit young to be a friend of my mom's." I try my best to cover my disappointment with a grin. I run my fingers through my wet hair. "It's nice to finally meet you. We seem to keep missing each other at family events."

"Yeah," she smiles. She shakes her head and mimicking my movement by tucking a strand of dark hair behind her ear. The movement makes her sweater stretch over her chest, and my whole body throbs.

Congratu-fucking-lations little brother.

"I should probably..." She points her thumb over her shoulder.

"Yeah, I gotta..." I gesture to my body. I'm still only wearing a towel, with freezing-cold drops of water covering my torso. Farrah laughs, her cheeks reddening again. She flicks those enchanting eyes up towards mine again.

"See you in there."

"I hope so," I say without thinking. Her eyes widen and her blush deepens. A smile twitches at her lips and then she turns towards the door. I watch her walk out, and then head to the window to see her jog across the yard towards the house. When she disappears through the patio doors, I let out a huge sigh.

Well, *fuck*. The first woman I've been attracted to in months also happens to be my brother's new fiancée.

You can get Engaged to Mr. Wrong by visiting this URL:

https://www.amazon.com/dp/B07MKTP2NX

Remember, sign up for my newsletter and get exclusive access to the Lilian Monroe Freebie Central. You'll get access to bonus content from all my books, regular updates and new release alerts.

http://eepurl.com/ddxnWL

Thank you so much for reading!
xox Lilian

Made in the USA
Lexington, KY
08 June 2019